The Lost Princes of Ambria

Royal fathers in search of brides!

Come to the breathtaking land of Ambria and
get swept up in Raye Morgan's captivating
world of feel-good fantasy as you fall in
love with royal daddies who juggle duty,
fatherhood—*and finding their perfect wives!*

Secret Prince, Instant Daddy!
Single Father, Surprise Prince!
Crown Prince, Pregnant Bride!
The Reluctant Princess
Pregnant with the Prince's Child
Taming the Lost Prince

All Available Now

Dear Reader,

This is the last book of a series of six about the Lost Princes of Ambria—a lovely, fog-shrouded, fictitious island nation off the coast of Western Europe. All the princes have been found and brought back home again. Their family, which was shattered and torn apart when their parents were killed by the Granvilli rebellion almost thirty years ago, is reconnected and healed about as well as it can be. Goodness and mercy are back in the land.

Too bad all our problems can't be solved so easily—but then, we're not royal, are we?

Last year we saw the Westminster Abbey wedding of Prince William and beautiful Kate Middleton, and all the excitement and celebration that surrounded it. This wonderful couple brought back star power to the British monarchy—a sense of special magic that reminds us why fairy tales so often feature princes and princesses. Larger than life, the focus of dreams. No wonder we love it all.

Prince Max and the woman he loves, who is secretly raising his child, need a bit of that magic to find their happy ending. They have to struggle through misunderstandings, a kidnapping and a heavy shared sadness that almost destroys their love. I hope you enjoy being a witness to the way they manage to capture their dream.

Thank you for reading my story.

Regards,

Raye Morgan

RAYE MORGAN

Taming the Lost Prince

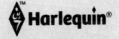

TORONTO NEW YORK LONDON
AMSTERDAM PARIS SYDNEY HAMBURG
STOCKHOLM ATHENS TOKYO MILAN MADRID
PRAGUE WARSAW BUDAPEST AUCKLAND

Recycling programs
for this product may
not exist in your area.

ISBN-13: 978-0-373-74175-5

TAMING THE LOST PRINCE

First North American Publication 2012

Copyright © 2012 by Harlequin Books S.A.

Raye Morgan has been a nursery school teacher, a travel agent, a clerk and a business editor, but her best job ever has been writing romances—and fostering romance in her own family at the same time. Current score: two boys married, two more to go. Raye has published more than seventy romance novels, and claims to have many more waiting in the wings. She lives in Southern California, with her husband and whichever son happens to be staying at home at the moment.

Books by Raye Morgan

PREGNANT WITH THE PRINCE'S CHILD*
THE RELUCTANT PRINCESS*
CROWN PRINCE, PREGNANT BRIDE!*
SINGLE FATHER, SURPRISE PRINCE!*
SECRET PRINCE, INSTANT DADDY!*
BEAUTY AND THE RECLUSIVE PRINCE
THE ITALIAN'S FORGOTTEN BABY

*The Lost Princes of Ambria

Other titles by this author available in ebook format.

This book is dedicated to Nick and Jenn, and most of all to CB, the new prince in our family.

CHAPTER ONE

PRINCE MAX leaned out over the edge of the wrought-iron rail on the balcony. A light rain was falling but he hardly noticed. He was at least the equivalent of five floors up. The castle garden below looked farther away than that. A strange, shivering impulse inside made him wonder what would happen if he jumped.

Too late now. A few weeks ago he could have jumped. He could have ended his worthless life with a flourish. No one would have cared.

But now he had a new life—new responsibilities. People were beginning to expect things of him. What the hell made them think he could possibly deliver?

Actually, this might be a better time to jump. Maybe he would find out he could fly. It looked so simple. All he had to do was spread his wings. He knew what it felt like to fly. He'd been flying ancient crates from past wars for years now. Flying planes was the one thing he knew he was good at. But taking that leap on his own would be different.

No, he wasn't going to jump. He wasn't going to mock his fate by trying to fly without a plane. Self-destruction wasn't really his style. But he did have a peacock feather he'd picked up in the castle gardens. He held it out.

"Fly and be free," he muttered to it. And then he let it go. It began its long, meandering flight toward the ground and he leaned out even farther, watching it go. It flashed back colors, blue and green and gold. As it neared the ground, it started to spin crazily. He laughed. "Go, baby," he murmured to it. "Do your thing."

The feather hit the ground and his laughter faded away. Now it was caught, just like he was. A short flight to nowhere.

"Hey," a candy-coated feminine voice said to him. "Don't lean out so far. You'll fall."

He closed his eyes for a moment. Was he ready for this? Did he need it?

"You okay, mister?" she said.

He turned slowly, wondering if she realized who he was. Probably not. He was dressed for hiking, not for the ball. But he thought he'd seen her before, passed her in the halls. He recognized the look. And he knew the drill. Either he gave her a simple friendly nod and went on his way, or he smiled at her suggestively and things went on from there. His choice. He could tell she was ready. Eager even. A part of him groaned.

But he couldn't give in to that. What the hell? He was young. Life was there to be lived. And who knew how much longer he'd be free to follow where his urges led him?

"I'm fine," he said, and he smiled.

"You're wet," she countered flirtatiously.

He shook his head like a sheepdog. Water flew everywhere. She gave a little shriek and then she laughed.

"You'd better come on to my place and get dry," she offered.

"Your place?" he repeated questioningly.

"Sure. My room is on this floor. I'm only a few doors away. You need to dry off. You wouldn't want to catch a cold, would you?"

His gaze made an exploratory journey down the length of her, from her spiked, fire-engine-red hair, down to her full lips, lingering on her hourglass figure. His look was insolent. He knew it. And he also knew she was the type of woman who liked that sort of thing.

"Sure, why not?" he said. Anything was better than joining the other royals at this ridiculous ball the queen had cooked up. A few hours with this willing playmate might be just the thing to help him get rid of this feeling of doom that was hanging over him. "You're like an angel of mercy, aren't you? Always on the lookout for someone in trouble."

Her smile had a wicked sparkle to it. "Not really," she said. "I'm kind of picky about who I help."

He raised an eyebrow. "And I made the grade?"

Her eyes widened appreciatively. "Oh, yeah. You'll do."

He pretended to bow. "I'm honored."

She giggled and led the way.

Queen Pellea swept into the royal office and glared at Kayla Mandrake. "So where is he?" she demanded.

Kayla jumped up from her desk, shaking her head. That sinking feeling she'd been fighting since she'd found out who the new prince actually was had come back with a vengeance. "I haven't seen him at all," she said. "I thought he was supposed to be here...."

Pellea grabbed the back of a chair, her knuckles white. "Of course he was. He was given complete instructions. And he blew them off, as usual. Everyone is waiting in the ballroom."

"Shall I make an announcement over the speaker system?"

Pellea looked pained. "Oh, Kayla, you've been in Paris all this time and you don't know how things have been. This guy is driving me crazy."

Kayla held back a grin. That was Max. He drove everyone crazy.

"He'll settle down," she told the queen without really believing it herself. "Once he understands the way we do things."

"The more he understands, the more he flouts the rules. You're going to have to go out and track him down."

Pellea made a sound of angry impatience and tossed her head in frustration. She was wearing a spectacular gown—deep blue silk threaded with gold, strapless, form-fitting, with a skirt cut to move sinuously as she danced…or walked. Kayla felt frumpy in her simple skirt and sweater.

"And I hope you're prepared to kill him when you find him," Pellea said dramatically.

"Your Majesty," Kayla began, beginning to give in to a touch of anxiety. She was trying to think of a new excuse for him on the fly—but something that wouldn't get her fired. The queen did have her emotional moments.

"Don't." Pellea held up a hand like a crossing guard. "I don't want to hear any tales of woe. I don't want to hear explanations and confessions. All I want is Prince Maximillian here where I can punish him."

She shivered with what looked like antic-ipation. "Or his head on a platter. That would do." Her dark eyes flashed. "Do you understand?"

Kayla nodded. Despite everything, she was working hard to suppress a grin. She didn't dare let it show. Pellea was so angry.

The trouble was, she knew very well that the Max she had known was sure to make Pellea even angrier as time went by. There was nothing she could do to avoid it.

"Yes, Your Majesty. I'll do my best."

"Just find him!"

Queen Pellea swept out like the storm she could sometimes resemble. Kayla took a deep breath and steadied herself. What now? How was she supposed to find a rebel prince who obviously didn't want to be found?

It was always this way with Max. Rules were made for other people, not for him. He was easily the most infuriating—and the most charming—man she'd ever known. Just the thought that she would see him again any moment gave her a thrill that was electric. But it also gave her a dull, pounding headache. How was she going to work this? Heaven only knew.

She started by making a few phone calls. There were guards everywhere and security officers working the monitors at special locations. If he was in the castle, someone must have seen him. And some had. She got a lead here and there, and finally, an actual sighting from a hall guard who'd seen him disappear into the apartment of a local girl who was well-known for partying.

"Of course," Kayla muttered acidly. "I should have known."

She started off toward the place like a rocket, but deep in her heart, she dreaded the whole confrontation ahead of her. What was she going to do once she got to the door? Barge in on a seduction? She shuddered as she punched in the floor designation on the elevator panel.

"Darn you, Max," she whispered. "Do you always have to make life so hard?"

She thought about the last time she'd seen him, almost two years ago, his thick, bronzed hair disheveled, his eyes bleary with pain. Emotional pain. They'd both been in agony that night, both mourning over the same tragedy. The next thing she'd known, he was gone.

The elevator doors slid open silently and she stepped off, heart beating, head aching. It was only a few steps to the doorway. She stood in front of it, wishing she were anywhere else. Her phone buzzed and she pulled it open. It was Pellea, of course.

"Yes?"

"Have you found him yet?"

She sighed. "I've got his location. I'm about to go in and see…."

"Watch him," Pellea warned. "If there's a balcony, he'll jump."

Kayla gasped. "You don't think he's suicidal, do you?"

"Oh, heavens no. He defies death for the fun of it. I swear he's got to be an adrenaline freak."

Kayla considered that seriously. "You know…" she began.

But Pellea wasn't waiting to hear other views.

"Last week, we had a gathering of the new princes at the ski chalet, a meeting for them to get to know each other better. We'd barely begun cocktails when Max and the chalet manager's two beautiful daughters took off on snowmobiles, racing off into the mountains as though it were nothing more than a free snow day. And they didn't come back."

"Oh."

"No excuses the next day, of course. He thinks his smile covers all bases."

"I see," she said for lack of anything cogent to add. She felt a little lost with the queen battering her with complaints like this. A part of her wanted to defend him, but how did you defend behavior like this?

"Last night it was dinner with the Italian ambassador. We're about to sign an important treaty with them. He didn't show. And what was the excuse? He'd stopped in at a pub and got involved in judging a karaoke contest and lost track of time."

"Oh, Max," Kayla said in soft despair.

"So I say, watch the balcony. He'll tie a rope to the edge and pretend he's Tarzan. Don't let him get away."

"I won't." She only wished her determination was as stout as it sounded.

Pellea sighed. Maybe her tone hadn't

been convincing. "Give me your exact location. I sent a couple of security officers up to help you. I'll key in directions for them."

That startled her. "Help me do what?" she asked after giving the queen her location.

"Make sure he doesn't escape. We'll tie him up and drag him in if we have to."

"We will?" She knew Max and she was pretty sure that wasn't going to be done easily. This whole thing was beginning to resemble a nightmare. She stared at the door to the target apartment. Max was supposedly in there. They'd told her he'd gone in with a woman. Did the phrase *love nest* come to mind? This wasn't the way she'd imagined their reunion might pan out.

"Now I want you to be forceful," Pellea encouraged. "You must take him by surprise."

Kayla gasped in horror as a picture of what that might mean spun through her head. "You mean…burst in on him without warning?"

"If you have to. Whatever you do, you've got to stop him from disappearing again. Call me when it's over."

"Yes, Your Majesty. Of course." She hung up just as two security guards stepped off the elevator and marched over to join her.

"Sgt. Marander, ma'am, at your service," the one who seemed to be in charge announced. "Here's the master key. We're here to back you up. We'll be right behind you."

She chewed on her lower lip. "Can I knock first?" she asked, rather forlorn.

His stare was steely cold. "I'm afraid not. Her Majesty specifically recommended a surprise attack. She's afraid he'll…"

"Escape by jumping off the balcony. Yes, she told me as much."

He glanced at her and frowned. He probably heard the reluctance in her voice and didn't approve. "Sorry, miss. Instructions from the queen are not to be taken lightly."

She took a deep breath. "All right," she said, straightening her shoulders and heading for the door. "Here I go."

She closed her eyes and turned the key in the door, letting it swing open. "Max?" she asked breathlessly, not daring to look. "Are you in there?"

There was an ominous moment of startled silence and then a deep voice cried, "Kayla! What are you doing here?"

She forced herself to squint through one slightly opened eye. And there he was, standing before her, completely clothed. Very civilized. Not scary at all. She gasped in relief.

"Oh, Max," she said, half laughing. And as he threw his arms around her, she sighed and went limp in his embrace. "I can't believe it's really you."

He hugged her, kissed each cheek, dropped a quick one on her lips and, finally, leaned back to take a look.

"Hey, gorgeous, it's been almost two years, hasn't it?"

She nodded, her head swimming. He was still the most beautiful man she'd ever seen, still hard and handsome, still looking like a playful rascal and a bit of a rogue. His thick rust-colored hair seemed to have a constant breeze blowing through it, his mischievous blue eyes were framed by eyelashes so thick it was almost criminal, and his mouth looked so deliciously sensual, it ought to be censored. That was Max, just as she remembered him. Lord, how she'd missed him!

"So what are you doing here?" he asked, looking completely bemused.

"I came to...to sort of arrest you. In a way." She made a face. What a farce.

"Arrest me?" At last he focused on the security guards behind her. He frowned. "What did I do now?"

"Oh, Max," she sighed. "Why can't you be good?"

"Kayla, my sweet," he said grinning at her, "you know that's not in my nature."

But he was genuinely happy to see her. Taking her in was like a good shot of whiskey. One look and he was transported two years back in time, back to those sidewalk cafés with the red umbrellas along the Mediterranean coast, back to the balmy breezes and sunlight filtering through the palms, back to hearing suggestive songs played by small combos while they'd sat sipping chichis, the local drink that tasted a bit like a Mai Tai and packed a punch like an angry kangaroo. The things they'd done, the things that had happened, the choices made, the regrets—it all still churned inside him. He couldn't let it go.

But he also couldn't regret knowing Kayla. She'd always been a joy. It was fantastic seeing her again.

"This is Kayla," he said casually to the redhead who was standing behind him, looking terrified. It appeared she wasn't used to having castle security barge in through her locked door. "Her husband was my best buddy in the old days when we flew sorties out of Trialta together."

"Oh," the redhead said weakly. Her teeth seemed to be chattering. "Nice to meet you, I'm sure."

"Yes," Kayla responded and tried to smile at the girl.

Max saw the confusion in her eyes and realized she was still digesting the situation she'd burst in on. It was pretty obvious she thought she'd found him having a "moment" here. That was hardly the case, though the redhead seemed to have thought it might turn into one, too.

But he hadn't been able to conjure up any interest. He'd been polite. He'd chatted. He'd accepted one small drink and the redhead had worked hard at creating a seductive scene. But he'd found himself looking out at the stars in the inky sky and listening to the strains of the orchestra from below in the ballroom, and all desire for that sort of satisfaction had melted away.

But before he found a way to explain all that, the two guards stepped forward and began to slip metal restraints on his wrists.

He looked down, startled. "What the hell is this?"

"Sir," Sgt. Marander said in an unfortunately pompous tone, "consider yourself in the custody of castle security."

Max blinked. He couldn't accept this. Handcuffs? They had to be kidding. He quickly saw two or three ways out of the situation. He could easily handle the guards and…

But then he looked up and met Kayla's worried gaze. Her pretty face, her dark, clouded eyes and her long, silky blond hair all created in flesh a picture that had haunted him for two years. Adrenaline still sizzled inside him for a few seconds, then began to drain away.

He wasn't going to run from Kayla. Now

that he'd found her again, he didn't want to lose her until they'd had a chance to talk. If he could mine her memories and join them with his, maybe he could slay some of the demons that kept him awake at night. Maybe.

"Please, Max," she was saying, reaching out and putting a hand on his arm. "It's really important to Queen Pellea that you make an appearance at the ball."

He smiled down into her anxious gaze. "There is nothing I'm looking forward to more," he lied smoothly. "Now that you're here, I'll have someone to dance with."

She jerked back, pulling her hand away. "Oh, no. Not me. You're supposed to be meeting eligible ladies of rank. That's not me."

He stared at her. "Kayla, what's the deal? Do you work for the royal family, or what?"

She nodded. "Yes. I've known the queen since we were kids together and my sister's husband is in the guard. Pellea offered me a job and I jumped at it." She shrugged, palms up. "I love it here."

He frowned, not sure what to make of that. When they'd been in Trialta, he'd assumed she was as much of a vagabond as he was. Now to know she had royal ties…

But what was he thinking? He was the one who was supposed to be a prince.

Still, he didn't like being corralled this way. He could tolerate going to the ball if they let him come on his own terms. This way was just too much. Kayla or no Kayla, he was back to wanting to get the hell out of here. But his hesitation had meant he was locked up.

"Hey, I'll come with you willingly," he noted. "But could we get rid of these handcuffs?"

She hesitated, looking down at them. Then she gazed up into his eyes.

He smiled. She sighed.

"Sure," she said, wondering if she were risking everything but hardly caring. She looked at the security agents. "Let him go."

The sergeant glared at her. "But, Miss…"

"I'll take the responsibility," she said. "If he bolts, I'll tell the queen it was my fault."

The man shrugged and used the key, but he didn't look happy about it.

Max smiled and flexed his wrists and looked toward the balcony in the redhead's room. He could make it in two bounds and be jumping for freedom in seconds. Everything in him was ready to go. Why the hell should he stick around when he knew he was going to hate the results?

CHAPTER TWO

KAYLA could read Max's mind. She knew him too well. She saw the glance as a way out and she moved in smoothly, taking his hand in hers, lacing their fingers together. If he was going to run for it, he was going to have to drag her with him.

"You're all mine now," she told him archly. "I'm calling the shots."

"Is that right?" he said, looking skeptical, but amused. "I thought I was the one who was supposed to be royal all of a sudden." He raised one quizzical eyebrow. "You've heard, haven't you? Now they've got me pegged as one of the lost princes. Can you believe it?"

She shook her head, smiling at him. "I'm finding it hard. When I realized it was you…" She shrugged and closed her eyes as she relived those moments, and when she spoke again, her voice was shaky. "Max, I thought you were dead."

He looked at her for a moment, then managed a crooked smile. "Which time?" he asked softly.

Her phone buzzed. She knew it was the queen. Pressing her lips together, she shook her head.

"We'll have to talk later." She reached for her phone but she didn't let go of his hand. She'd learned a lesson or two over the years, and one of them was to look both ways before stepping off the curb.

"Yes, Your Majesty. We're on our way."

Ten minutes later they were in Pellea's public parlor while she flitted about and generally let Max know he was on thin ice with her. Kayla watched, but hardly listened. She knew the queen was crazy about him and was just trying to convince him to behave.

At the same time, she herself was a bit impatient with all this. She felt as though every nerve ending was vibrating right now. There were so many things to take care of, so much to consider. Max was back and she had to figure out how to fit him into her life again. She had a thousand questions for him. There was so much she wanted to know, so much they'd missed. So much they needed to discuss.

For instance, had he come close to marrying anyone in the last two years? Was there someone out there? She was hoping there was, but the signs weren't good. If he had someone serious in his life, she could move on without any lingering doubts. Couldn't she?

The funny thing was, she couldn't imagine him married. He didn't have a married way about him. His beautiful eyes had a look that said he was always searching for something and not very satisfied with what he'd found. You had a sense that there was something missing in his life, but he wasn't sure what it was and he knew he hadn't seen it yet. Just seeing that in him scared her.

But the queen seemed to have no forbearance left for all that. She knew what she wanted from Max and she wanted it now.

"The first thing we're going to do is get

you into some decent clothes," she said, rummaging through her closet.

"What? You don't like my style?" He said it in a tone that might have seemed insolent if he hadn't paired his words with a look of pure innocence that caught Pellea by surprise, making her laugh.

"Now I see what the problem is," she told him, shaking her head. "You just don't know any better. You need to learn a thing or two about being a prince, don't you?"

"If you insist." His mouth twisted but he bent forward in a sweeping bow. "Anything for you, my beautiful queen."

Despite everything, Pellea colored slightly, then glanced Kayla's way. "You've got to admit, the boy's a charmer," she said out of the side of her mouth. "I think he's a diamond in the rough, too. We'll see what we can make of him." She smirked. "Heat and pressure. That's how you get perfect diamonds. Are you game?"

He didn't answer but she'd already turned away and was hunting through a closet again, muttering about sizes and ruffled shirts.

He looked at Kayla and shrugged, as

though to say, "They've got me this time," and she smiled at him, her heart full of affection for all he'd meant to her in the past. She wasn't sure what the future would bring. But things were never dull when Max was around.

Her smile faded as she remembered that there was something more lasting than memories between them, something more precious than life itself. And that was when she decided it was time for her to go.

"Your Majesty, if you don't need of me here…"

Pellea poked her head back out of the closet. "Go ahead, Kayla," she said. "I know you've got work to do. I won't keep you."

"Thank you," Kayla said, then she turned and gave Max a stern look. "You will be good, won't you?"

"At what?" he teased with a lopsided smile.

She glared at him. "The guard is outside so don't think you can get away with anything," she murmured to him out of Pellea's hearing.

He gave her a "Who? Me?" look. She shook

her head and started for the door. "Have a lovely time at the ball," she said over her shoulder. "I'm sure you'll be the star."

And she was out the door before he had a chance to say or do anything else.

She hurried back to the office, hoping to get some work done that she'd neglected while she was off chasing princes. It had been a hectic week. Pellea had sent her to represent the DeAngelis royal family at a financial conference in Paris. She'd hated leaving for a whole week, but the fact that the queen had that much faith in her had been wonderful. She'd worked herself to the bone trying to live up to expectations and she was exhausted.

And while she was gone, the search for the last of the lost princes of Ambria had struck gold. First Mykal Marten, whom she'd met before she left for the continent, had been confirmed as the fourth prince. And then the news had come that the fifth and last prince had been discovered. When she saw the name—Max Arragen—in a newspaper account, she hadn't thought much of it, but then she saw a picture. It was blurry and taken from a distance, but

the jaunty set of the shoulders had made
her think of Max—her Max. She'd gasped
and begun to wonder.

It wasn't until she'd returned home to
Ambria a day ago that she'd seen a good
picture and realized that Prince Max
really was the man she'd known in Trialta
as Max Arragen two years before. And that
sent her into a virtual tailspin.

She'd only known him for about six
months, but the time they'd spent together
had been crazy and intense. He was her
husband's best friend, and they'd both been
working as contract pilots, flying reconnaissance missions against the tyranni-
cal regime of the North African nation of
Trialta on the Mediterranean. They'd lived
like young people involved in war often
do, working hard during the day, partying
at night like there was no tomorrow. They
were fighting for the rebels and thought
they were invincible.

She couldn't believe he was back in her
life again—at least in a peripheral way.
He always managed to inject excitement
and surprise into everything, like no one
else she'd ever known. She remembered

times in Trialta where it had seemed she and Eddie were in the lead vehicle in a continuous car chase—and Max was at the wheel.

And then came the day when Eddie didn't return from a mission. The wreckage of his plane was found, and all the parties stopped. Kayla had clung to Max at the time and they'd mourned together, hardly believing that the Eddie they both loved so much could be gone forever. No one else could have understood how deep their grief was.

But that was then. Things had changed, for both of them. Surely he'd had some life-changing experiences since she last knew him. And she'd had a beautiful, wonderful child.

What would it be like to be friends with Max now? She was a little bit afraid to find out. She wasn't the wide-eyed innocent she'd been two years before. She had some secrets of her own. And how would she keep them from him, now that he was going to be living right here in the castle?

She buried her worries in work, staying an hour longer than normal. And then, once she'd put away her papers and shut off her computer, she gave in to temptation and made her way down to the ballroom instead of going straight to her room.

She took a back entrance and climbed the stairs to a seldom-used interior balcony that overlooked the entire floor area. The orchestra was playing a waltz and the couples swept across the floor, around and around, the women like flowers in their beautiful dresses, the men resplendent in gold-edged uniforms of white or blue or crimson. Despite everything, it took her breath away and made her heart beat faster. A scene like this would make anyone want to be noble, especially if they'd been raised on fairy tales.

She watched for a few minutes longer, caught up in the magic. How wonderful to be royal and to live as though you were the star of it all. Just being here in the castle made her feel as though she were blessed. But it also made her feel a new and more intense responsibility to her country and her people. She wondered if Max would start to feel a little of that soon.

She could pick out most of the princes.

So handsome, every one of them—so tall and strong. They looked like men who were confident in themselves and ready to take on the world. She could hardly believe Max was about to take his place alongside of them.

There was Prince Mykal, sitting on the sidelines, still recovering from a horrendous motorcycle accident from a few months before. Prince David, one of her favorites, was dancing with beautiful Ayme, who had recently become his bride. Prince Joe, still looking like a California surfer with his sun-streaked hair, was laughing with Kelly, his own new bride. And newly crowned King Monte had Pellea in his arms and was leading her around the floor with such obvious passion, you'd think the honeymoon was starting that night. That made her laugh softly to herself.

She searched the crowd. Where was Max? Her gaze lingered a moment on Princess Kim. She was glad to see her looking happy after all that she'd been through on the enemy side of the island with the Granvilli partisans. It was good to have her safe

and sound, back in the castle where she belonged. But where was Max?

At first worried, she began to get angry.
If he had slipped away again…!

And then she saw him.

Max was standing with a group of men
she didn't recognize. As she watched, the
men moved away and a beautiful dark-
haired woman was brought up to be presented to him. Kayla felt a tug on her
heartstrings, but she tried desperately to
suppress it. She couldn't be jealous. There
was no sense behind it. She had to keep
it down. Max was not hers and never had
been. Never would be, especially now that
he was a prince. There was no justification
for any jealousy. She couldn't let it happen.

She watched as they danced. He moved
so well, as if he were floating on air. He
was talking to his partner and she was blos-
soming in his arms. He could have been
born for this—and of course, he really was!

The dance was over. She could breathe
again. And now, she really had to go. But
she watched for just one minute more, and
suddenly his head was tilted up. He was
looking right at her. And as she watched,

he lifted a glass of champagne and smiled at her, giving her a toast. Her breath caught in her throat and she gasped. He gave her a nod, and then a lascivious wink. Her face felt hot as she pulled back, away from where anyone could see her. She was laughing, though. That wink was guaranteed to keep her warm that night. Trust Max!

But as she turned and left the balcony, her amusement evaporated. She couldn't do this. She couldn't be watching Max from afar and reacting every time he noticed her. Nothing good could come of this. Much better that she should stay as far away from him as she could get. If he really wasn't attached, it would be his duty to find a bride as soon as possible. Watching him fall in love would be tough to take. And if he ever found out…

No, keeping in touch with Max was much too dangerous. She had to find a way to avoid it.

She hadn't eaten since breakfast and she was starving. Glancing at her watch, she knew it was too late to pick up Teddy before he went to sleep. Her heart ached as

she thought about that. She missed him.
Her baby was only a little over a year old
and she missed him when she had late
days like this. Sighing, she knew she had
to speak to Pellea about it. She really didn't
want to be away from her child this long.
At the same time, she was so lucky to have
this job...

She stopped in at the all-night café and
got a salad to eat once she got home.

Then she headed for her sister Caroline's
room, just two doors down from hers.

"Hi," she called softly, opening the door
with her own key. "How are they?"

"Sleeping like lambs," Caroline said, rising from the couch where she'd been reading and coming to give her sister a hug.

Just two years apart, they looked enough
alike that there was always someone who
asked if they were twins. Caroline wore
her blond hair short, pixie-style, and had
a more sleepy, languid look about her, but
otherwise, they were practically replicas
and had always been especially close.

They stood together looking down at
where the two little boys, one dark-haired

like his father, the other as blond as his mother, lay side by side, sound asleep.

Caroline's husband, Rik, was a rising star in the Ambrian royal guard. Right now he was on a mission on the Granvilli side of the island and would be gone for a few days. Luckily, whether Rik was home or not, Caroline loved having Teddy in to play with her own boy.

"Why don't you leave him here for the night?" she suggested. "He's used to sleeping here after the last week when you were in Paris. And it was so hard to put them down tonight, I hate to wake them up and have to start all over again."

"Are you sure?" Kayla felt guilty, but she was so tired, it sounded like a good thing to do.

"Absolutely. You're only two doors down. I can get you over here fast if I need you. Just come on over first thing in the morning and it will all be good."

She stayed for half an hour, sharing her salad with her sister while they talked, watching her baby while he slept.

And then she was back in the corridor, on her way home and looking down toward the public area, wondering how the ball was going. It was interesting to live this way, with everything happening so close at hand. The castle lifestyle was growing on her. She had been new to it a year before when she'd come to work here, but she was used to it now and it seemed a comfortable way of life. She compared it to living on a huge cruise ship.

She opened her own door and went in, yawning and kicking off her shoes as she did. A tap on a switch turned on a soft light in the kitchen, which did enough to light the path to her bedroom. She made her way slowly through the apartment, casting off clothes as she went, first her jacket, then her skirt, then her sweater.

She was thinking about crashing straight onto her bed and closing her eyes and not opening them again until morning. Heavenly peace. No dreams, please. Just wonderful sleep. Her eyes began to droop in anticipation.

But it was not to be. Two steps short of her destination, just as she was reaching back to unhook her bra, a dark hulk rose from her overstuffed chair in the corner.

"You know," the hulk said ruefully, "I'd love to let you go on with this, but I have a feeling you'd hate me in the morning. Just a hunch."

She screamed, grabbing her sweater back again and pressing it to her chest. At the same time, Max jumped forward and took her by the shoulders.

"No, don't scream," he said urgently. "I get into so much trouble when women scream."

She glared up at him, quickly pushing him away, startled and exasperated all at once. She could smell alcohol on his breath, but that was hardly surprising. Still, she was wary enough to be careful.

Handsome men, liquor and a moonlit night—the recipe for disaster.

"Then don't jump out at them from dark corners, maybe," she suggested sharply.

He shrugged as though anxious to make up for scaring her. "Okay, okay. It's a deal."

"Oh, Max." She glared at him as she tried to keep covered in all the most delicate areas. "Why did you let me get this far before you said anything?"

His eyebrows rose. "Are you kidding me?"

"Oh!" She shook her head, but she was calming down. "Look that way," she insisted, pointing to the wall. "And don't turn around until I tell you to."

He turned obediently and she began to search her drawer for fresh clothes to wear. "What are you doing here?" she demanded at the same time.

"I wanted to see you. We need some time to talk. Old times and all that."

She pulled on a comfortable top.

"Maybe call first next time," she suggested grumpily as she dug for something to pull over her legs. "How did you get in here anyway?"

He chuckled. "Princes pretty much rule around this castle. You tell people you're a prince and they want to do things for you. The housekeeper couldn't wait to do me a favor."

"That's a problem." She sighed. "Okay, you can turn around."

He turned and looked at her and he was knocked out. Here he'd just come from a royal ball filled with beautiful women who'd all spent half the day in the beauty shop and were dressed to kill and no one

he'd seen there turned him on the way
Kayla did wearing a simple sweatshirt and
black leggings, with her hair looking like
a tornado had just come through.

"I think I love you," he said, taking in
all her rumpled glory and smiling. "I know
I've missed you like crazy. It's so good to
see you again."

She gazed into his warm blue eyes and
melted. She knew he was kidding, that this
was his way of joking about emotions instead of dealing with them. But she also
knew he was recognizing the ties between
them and ready to embrace them, just like
it used to be.

Still, she had to wonder if he remembered that last night as clearly as she did.
He had done nothing to indicate it. As far
as she was concerned, she hoped he had a
touch of amnesia. That night had been a
crazy rush of pain and grief and anguish
and they hadn't handled it very well. Best
to forget it. If they could.

She gave herself a moment to really look
at him. Pellea had found him a striking
uniform to wear to the ball, but he'd taken
off the jacket and pulled open the shirt,

displaying some gorgeous skin and manly chest hair. Now he looked less than formal. She shook her head at the sight, but despite everything, she enjoyed seeing him. She always did.

"How did you get away from Pellea?"

He shrugged. "It wasn't easy. The woman was watching me like a hawk."

She sighed and sank into a chair, gesturing for him to sit on the couch across from her. "She'll probably be calling me any minute to organize a search party."

He moved her discarded jacket and dropped down onto the arm of the couch, then leaned toward her. "You won't give me up, will you?" he said with a puppy-dog look.

"Are you kidding?" she told him crossly. "Of course I will. I'm not risking my job so that you can play hooky."

He laughed. "Good point." Then he frowned. "What is your job exactly?"

"I'm the queen's personal assistant. I do whatever she needs to get done but doesn't have time to do herself."

It was a good job and she was proud of it. As a single mother without anyone to count on but herself, she was lucky to have it. If she ever lost it, for any reason, she would be in real trouble. There weren't many good jobs for women in Ambria right now and the queen was a wonderful woman to work for. With a two-year-old of her own, Pellea understood the problems Kayla had to face and was ready to give her a lot of leeway.

"Ah," Max said, "impressive. Quite another level from the job you had in Trialta."

She smiled, thinking of it. "Selling T-shirts to tourists from a kiosk on the beach. Yes, I didn't get much chance to show my skills and talents at that one."

But it hadn't mattered then. Her days were spent waiting for Eddie to come back from a flight, and her nights were filled with wine, music and friends. For a few months, life had been carefree and exciting. But you had to pay for everything, one way or another, and she'd been paying the price ever since.

Max was staring at her as though he could see what she was thinking. "And yet, here you are, barely two years later, assistant to the queen."

She gave him a look. "I do have a university education, you know."

He appeared surprised. "No, I didn't know. When did you get that?"

She smiled. "Long before I first met you."

"No kidding." He frowned, thinking that over. "That's more than I've got. And they think they want me to be a prince."

Her smile wavered a bit. It was true. From what she knew of his background, he might have a bit of trouble. He'd never been shy about it. While sipping drinks in the sidewalk cafés of Trialta, he'd regaled them with tales of his childhood living on the streets, always making it sound hilarious rather than tragic. But she'd often thought the raw tattered ghost of deprivation lingered in the shadows of his eyes.

He'd had a rough childhood. Any breaks he ever got he'd worked hard to achieve. That was very different from what most royals experienced. The newspaper accounts had filled in some of the parts of his background she hadn't known before, but she didn't know how accurate they were.

"From what I've read in the newspapers

and magazines, they seem to think that you were spirited off on the night of the rebellion," she said to him musingly. "When the Granvilli family attacked and burned the castle—when your parents, the king and queen were killed, and all the DeAngelis royal children went into hiding."

She shuddered just thinking of it. Those poor kids!

"Do you know how you escaped? Do you have any idea who it was who saved you by carrying you off that night?"

His shrug was careless, as if he didn't know and didn't really care. "Whoever they were, they didn't take very good care of me. By the time I was seven or eight, I was fending for myself on the streets. Before that, there were various strangers—at one point I think I was staying with a pickpocket who tried to teach me his tricks. But as far as I know, nobody was around for long at anytime. There's no one I can claim."

It broke her heart to think of a child being abandoned like that. She knew from his stories during their Trialta days that he'd been taken in by a fisherman for a while, but the man was cruel and he eventually ran away. It wasn't until his late teens when he was given a corner to sleep in and a job cleaning the chapel that he met a wonderful older man—a pastor—and his kindly wife, who made it their business to see that he was clothed and had a safe place to stay.

The pastor had a hobby of flying ancient aircraft—planes from twentieth century wars. Pretty soon he was teaching Max the ropes, introducing him to aviation, and after that life was much brighter. Max joined the Ambrian Air Force as soon as he was old enough. And that was pretty much all she knew.

"And no one ever guessed you were one of the lost princes," she murmured, looking at him wonderingly.

He laughed shortly. "Did you guess?"

She spread her hands out. "No."

"Neither did I. That shows you how long the odds were."

"Yes." She sighed. "How horrible for you to be treated like that as such a young child. I'm glad the Granvillis are paying the price for their treason now."

He stirred restlessly. "That's life. Sometimes you win, sometimes you lose."

"And sometimes they pull the chair out from under you, just when you think they've given you a throne to sit on."

He grinned at her appreciatively. "A cautionary tale, Kayla? Reminding me not to count on anything?"

She nodded. She couldn't help it. She'd always been a cautious one. Her only times of going crazy had involved marrying a flyer and then letting grief make her lose all control when he died. "Count no chicks before they hatch."

He cocked his head to the side. "Wisdom as well as beauty."

"Nice of you to notice." She rose, feeling a little too nervous to sit for long. "Would you like a drink? Iced tea? A cup of coffee?"

"A beer?" he suggested, following her to the little kitchenette.

"I think I have one." And she did, ice cold and ready to drink. She pulled it out of the refrigerator and popped the top for him.

He took a long sip, sighed with satisfaction and leaned against the counter, looking at her. "So what have you been doing all this time?" he asked her. "You didn't come straight here from Trialta did you?"

"No. I've been here for less than a year."

"And what were you doing before that?"

She hesitated. Her heart was thumping in her chest. It was time to come clean. She had to tell him. He would find out soon enough anyway. And if he thought she were trying to keep it from him, he might think...

She shivered.

"I...uh...I had a baby." She forced herself to look him in the eye and not waver. "A little boy. I call him Teddy."

"Teddy?" He blinked at her.

"Yes. He's at my sister's right now, down the hall. Maybe you can meet him tomorrow."

And she stared into his eyes, searching for doubt, searching for memories, searching for anything that would tell her he'd guessed the truth.

CHAPTER THREE

MAX's reaction came a beat too late. Kayla knew he'd had a quick second to think before he let his natural instincts take over. What was he thinking in that flash of time? What was he feeling? His crystal-blue eyes didn't show a thing. But that tiny hesitation did.

"Teddy," he said, sounding pretty normal. "You named him after Eddie, huh? Great."

He licked his upper lip quickly, then smiled and reached out to give her a one-armed hug. "Kayla, I'm so glad you have a piece of Eddie to hold on to. That is very cool."

He was looking right into her eyes now, seeming completely sincere. "I can hardly wait to meet him."

Glancing down, she realized, to her horror, that her fingers were trembling. Quickly, she shoved them under the hem of her sweatshirt.

"How about you?" she said, a little breathless. "I guess you're not married."

"Married!" His laugh was short and humorless. "You know me better than that."

"If Pellea has her way, you soon will be."

His deep, painful groan made her smile.

"Did you meet anyone interesting at the ball?"

"That wasn't all the ball was about, was it?" His groan was louder this time. "Oh, lord, do you think she's going to have more of them?"

"Of course. You have to marry someone. The others are all paired up already. Pellea wants to get you settled as well."

His sigh was heartfelt as he leaned wearily across the little counter. "Why don't you marry me? Then we can forget all about this nonsense and just be happy."

She looked away. The very suggestion sent something skittering through her like sparks from fireworks and she took a quick, gasping little breath, trying to suppress the feeling.

Marrying Max—what a concept. Luckily, that would never happen, not even for the sake of convenience. There was no way Max could ever take care of her and her baby. It wouldn't work. She'd been out in the world with him and she probably knew him better than she knew any other man, other than her husband. Max was born to be a bachelor.

Even Eddie had said so. "Max will never get married," he'd told her when she tried to have a go at a little matchmaking at one point. "He's like those animals that die in captivity. They can't be tamed. They can't even be gentled. Leave Max alone. He'll just break their hearts. And yours, too.'"

Eddie was right, as usual. Max was not a man to hang your heart on. She shook her head and got up the nerve to meet his gaze again. "Sorry, Max. You're going to have to walk that lonesome valley on your own."

His mouth twisted with a bit of pretended chagrin, but he wasn't really thinking about what she'd said. His gaze was skimming over her face, searching in her eyes, looking for something in the set of her lips. She wasn't sure what he expected to see, but it was disturbing, and she turned away, heading back to the living room.

She could feel him watching her, as though his gaze were burning a brand into her back. She forced herself not to look, and finally he came after her and sank onto the couch.

"Come and sit down by me," he said.

His voice was low and there was a new element in it...something different, something mysterious. She felt wary and her pulse stuttered and then began to move a bit faster. There was a sense of being a bit off-kilter. Somehow, the room seemed warmer. A new tension quivered in the air. Every time her eyes met his, the tension seemed thicker, more insistent, like a drumbeat beginning to make itself heard across a rain-forest jungle.

She took a deep breath and held it for a moment, trying to calm herself. They were just friends, but she worried that he might be edging toward something more. She couldn't let that happen. Not again.

"Come on," he coaxed. He wasn't smiling but his gaze was warm. Almost smoldering.

She shook her head and dropped back into the chair. "No. I think I'll stay here."

"What's the matter?" he asked her.

She licked her dry lips. "I think we need to keep a demilitarized zone between us," she said, trying to sound casual and friendly at the same time.

His eyebrows shot up. "What are you talking about?"

She took a deep breath. How to begin?

"I'm serious, Max. I don't think we ought to be close. You're moving into a whole different sphere of life. I don't belong there. Let's not start anything that will have to be..." She shrugged, not sure she wanted to put it into words.

His bright gaze clouded and he appeared bewildered by what she'd said. "But you seem a part of this castle stuff and I'm just a beginner," he pointed out. "What are you talking about with this 'different sphere' business?"

She wondered for just a moment if he were really that naive about the class structure in their society. Ambria had always been a remote, self-absorbed little kingdom. Islands tended to breed peculiarities in animals and people if they were cut off from the mainstream for too long. Now that the monarchy had taken back control, after a twenty-five-year exile, and some of the old customs and rituals were being revived.

Royalty was royalty. It was special. That was all part of establishing authority and building back the old foundations. They were meant to be set apart from the common Ambrian. That was just the way it had to be.

"I'm an employee," she told him cheerfully. "You're a prince. Never the twain shall meet."

He made a face as though he thought that was complete tripe, but he would accept her judgment for the moment.

"We can still be friends, can't we? We can still talk."

"Sure."

He frowned. "I'm counting on you for that, you know."

That was just the problem. "Max..."

He took in a deep breath. "Here's the

deal, Kayla. I don't know what I'm doing here." His gaze was hard now, insistent, and yet at the same time, completely vulnerable. "I don't know if I can stand too much of this prince stuff. It's not me."

"Oh." A flash close to pain went through her. He thought he couldn't do this. And yet, how could she be surprised? This was exactly what she would have expected if anyone had asked her. But that didn't mean she could let him go down this road without a struggle. He had to see how important it was.

"I'm willing to give it a go. For now. But I'm not feeling too confident. Most of my life has been lived on the other side of the divide. I don't know if I can adapt."

"Of course you can." She wished she could find the words she needed to get through to him. "Max, you were meant to be a prince from the beginning. Don't you see? The part where you lived on the streets was the mistake."

"I'm not so sure about that." He winced, then went on softly, his eyes looking dark and luminous, his voice barely hiding the years of uncertainty he'd lived through.

"Sometimes I think I never got a family because I didn't deserve one. I was a misfit. A pretty bad misfit. And maybe I didn't ever get that kind of family love because..." He looked up and met her gaze. "Because I'm just unlovable."

She gasped. He wasn't joking. His expression was serious, questioning. Now she had to stop herself from going to him, from sliding down beside him and pushing away his pain with her arms. And at the same time, everything in her wanted to do it.

"Max! How can you say that? Women adore you!"

He stared at her for a moment, then gave a half laugh, half grunt. "That's not love, Kayla. That's something else."

Her head went back in surprise. Who would have believed Max would be the one to see the difference so clearly? But still, he seemed to be utterly blind to his own strengths. He was always so carefree and debonair. She'd never known he had this insecurity at his core. She had to make him see how wrong it was.

"Oh, come on. What did we used to call

you? Mr. Casanova. A new girl on your arm every night."

His sigh was full of regrets. "You see, that's just it." He took a long drink from his beer and stared into space. "Lots of new girls. No true love."

It was hard to believe that a man this appealing, this attractive, thought he couldn't find his soul mate. She looked at him, so handsome, so adorable. Her fingers ached to run through that thick auburn hair. It took all her will to stay where she was.

"Haven't you ever been in love?" she asked him.

"Not really." He squinted at her, thinking it over. "I don't think so. Not like you and Eddie." His smile was crooked. "I used to watch you two together and I think I hated you almost as much as I loved you."

"Oh, Max…"

"You know what I mean. It was pure jealousy. You two were so good together, so…so devoted." His voice broke on the word and she had to close her eyes and bite her lip to keep from going to him.

Devoted. Yes, that was exactly the way it had been. When she'd found Eddie, she couldn't believe her luck. They'd met in an elevator in their apartment building in Paris. As they traveled up the floors, people got off, but the two of them remained, until they were alone and looking at each other tentatively across the empty car. Their eyes met. Love at first sight. And when they finally got to her floor, he admitted his had been four stops before. How could she not invite him in for a cup of coffee? Two months later, they were married.

When he'd died, she had thought life was over. She moved in a dark, menacing fog, blindly searching for some way out of the pain, not really believing it was possible. For days, she was obsessed, thinking of ways to join him. And then she realized she had someone else to think about.

"Do you remember...?" Max's voice choked.

She stiffened. Here it came. She had to keep a cool front. Still, she had to tell the truth, at least as far as it was safe.

"I remember too much," she said softly.

"Me, too." He finished off his beer and looked at her. "I think about Eddie every day."

She nodded, closing her eyes. "Me, too."

She wasn't going to cry. She had to hold it back. For a moment, she let herself recall the way it had been being married to Eddie. Sunshine every day. Champagne for breakfast. Walks on the beach and dancing barefoot to a reggae tune. Driving with the top down. Love in the afternoon. Eddie was the best. The very best.

But she couldn't let herself think about him too much. That was a temptation that could sap her life away.

"Remember that day we went sailing in the bay," he said, "and your straw hat flew off and Eddie and I jumped into the water and raced for it?"

She nodded, trying to smile. "We had a picnic on that little island and we ate all those cherries."

"And then spent an hour rolling in the sand, moaning, with the worst stomachaches imaginable."

She managed a half grin. "I thought we were going to die."

He laughed. "I wanted to die."

His words seemed to echo in the room.

Eddie was the one who had died, not long after that sunny day.

She closed her eyes again. They had to stop this. No good could come of it. They were laying treacherous emotional land mines all around. If they didn't stop, something was going to explode.

She wanted to stop. She tried. But somehow she couldn't keep the words from coming.

"I remember when you and Eddie would fly off into those big thunder clouds," she said softly, staring into the past, "like two falcons challenging the sky. It was so scary, but so magnificent. It made me shiver every time. I could hardly breathe. You were angels flying into the danger zone. And every time you came back victorious, another strike for the good guys, another strike for justice in the world." She turned to look at him, emotion almost choking her. "I was so proud of you both."

He didn't answer. Instead, he shook his head and looked away, and she knew his voice was probably too rough to use right now.

She should stop. She should push this

all away into the past. But she couldn't. It was as though she had to get this out in the open in order to let it go. She tried not to say anything more, but the words came anyway.

"Everyone was proud of you. You were heroes. The best. The brightest stars."

She swallowed hard, then reached out across the coffee table and took his hand.

"And then, on that dark, rainy day in November, you took off together, as usual, but you...you came back alone."

She blinked, wondering why there were no tears in her eyes. She usually had tears by now when she went over this in her own head. Why wasn't she crying?

"I stood there and watched your plane fly in, and I knew in my heart what it meant. But I didn't want to accept it. I kept thinking, no, he'll be coming. He's just had engine trouble or took a wrong turn or..." Her voice choked and she took a deep, shuddering breath. "I kept staring into the horizon, looking for that black spot to appear against the sky."

Her words seemed to echo against the

walls as they both sat quietly, waiting for the pain to fade.

"Eddie was the best guy I ever knew," he said at last, his voice rough as a rocky beach. "It should have been me."

"No…" She held his hand as tightly as she could, with both her own.

"He was true and honest and brave. Not like me."

"No," she said fiercely. "Don't ever say that."

His face was twisted with pain. "Kayla, Kayla, it should have been me."

She was next to him on the couch now, and she wasn't sure how she got there. But she had to be with him, as close as she could get. She had to remind him of his own worth, his own value. She couldn't let him feel this way.

She took his beautiful face between her hands and stared right into his eyes. "Eddie was a wonderful man. But so are you. You're just as good and precious and worthy."

He looked at her and winced, as though the light was too bright in that direction.

"I would trade it all to have him back again," he muttered.

She shook her head. "I don't think you can make bargains like that. I don't think you can trade yourself. What happens, happens. We have to use it to make ourselves into better people."

"Yeah." He tried to twist away from her, then gave it up. "But it shouldn't have been Eddie. Not Eddie."

Her fingers dug into his hair and he looked down into her eyes. He was going to kiss her. She knew it and she knew she should stop him. She tried. But as his arms slowly wrapped around her and he pulled her body close, she could only sigh and raise her mouth to find his.

The moment was electric. They'd come together as though it were inevitable, as though they were pulled by a force they weren't strong enough to fight. Everything in Kayla cried out with need for Max. In this primal moment, he was hers and she was ready to surrender again. Just like before. She clung to him, clung and arched into his embrace, waiting for the touch of his tongue.

His face came closer. She could feel his warm breath on her lips. Closing her eyes, she sighed and offered her face to him.

And that was when the door to the apartment flew open and Pellea came storming into the room like a Valkyrie.

The two of them stared at her, mouths hanging open in shock, still tangled in each others arms. She glared back, her hands on her hips as the door slammed shut behind her.

"What the heck is going on here?" she demanded.

Max frowned, not letting Kayla go. "Doesn't anyone ever knock in this place?" he quizzed right back at her.

"You're a fine one to talk," Kayla said, sotto voce.

Pellea's nostrils flared. "I knocked. Nobody answered. I guess you were too busy with this…this…" Her hand waved around in the air but she couldn't find a word that would suit. Still, her annoyance was clear.

Kayla began to pry herself loose from Max's octopus embrace and rose quickly in order to show respect for Pellea's position, hoping Max would notice and follow her lead.

"Oh, Pellea, don't get upset," she said, half laughing at the crazy situation. "We're old friends. Max was Eddie's best friend. They flew together in the Mediterranean."

Pellea's mouth made a round circle for a moment. She looked from one to the other of them. "Wow," she said. "I had no idea."

Kayla looked back at Max. He was grumpy and she couldn't really blame him. But she was glad Pellea had interrupted them. If anyone needed an intervention, it was the two of them. She gave him a look and he slowly rose beside her.

"I didn't realize he was the man I'd known until yesterday, when I first saw his picture in your office," Kayla explained.

Pellea frowned suspiciously. "You didn't say anything."

"I…I needed some time to get used to it. You see, earlier I had thought he'd been killed in Somalia months ago and…"

"Wait." Pellea held up her hand. "Your husband was killed flying for the Trialta National Forces, wasn't he?"

"Yes. He and Max flew together there."

Pellea looked skeptical. "And you never had any idea he might be royal?"

Kayla shook her head. "Never. I would have laughed at anyone who suggested it."

"Hey," Max complained in a low voice.

"Oh, never mind." Pellea looked at Max, then at Kayla, and shook her head and her look turned thoughtful. "That just makes it all more interesting, doesn't it?"

Kayla had to fight hard to resist rolling her eyes. "If you say so," she muttered, wondering what the queen had up her sleeve now.

She was carrying a portfolio, obviously something she'd brought in to show off for some reason. But her attention had been diverted. She glared at the recalcitrant prince.

"I feel like I'm going to have to put a homing device on you," she warned him.

He frowned, looking rebellious. He glanced at Kayla, then looked straight at the queen. "Is this prince job a twenty-four-hour commitment?" he asked suspiciously.

"Of course," Pellea said sharply.

"Of course not," Kayla said at the same time.

She certainly didn't want to contradict

the queen, but she thought they'd better widen the discussion a bit before Max said something he would regret. The look on his face already set the stage for handing in his resignation as a royal. She didn't think the queen should portray it with quite such a heavy hand. Talk about scaring the quarry away! A little finesse was in order.

"The other princes don't have homing devices," she explained sensibly.

Pellea frowned at her. "The other princes don't need them."

Kayla shrugged reluctantly. "Good point."

And don't you forget it, Pellea seemed to say with her flashing eyes, though not a word passed her lips. She turned to Max and her face softened.

"Did you enjoy the ball?" she asked him hopefully.

He hesitated. Kayla bit her lip and prayed. For once in his life, was he going to be good? She knew there was a struggle going on inside him.

"Yes, Your Majesty, I did," he admitted at last. "You put on an amazing show. I was impressed."

Pellea looked pleased. "There, you see?

If you would just relax and see what we're all about, you'll learn to love us in no time at all." She was smiling now, looking at both Kayla and Max with affection. "You'll see," she added, and then her smile faded and she took a deep, deep breath.

"But there's something else," she said, sliding the portfolio out from under her arm. "Take a look at this."

Sweeping aside the things on the coffee table, she pulled a poster out and spread it out on the flat surface.

"All right," she said dramatically, looking at Max. "Now explain this, mister!"

Max and Kayla stepped closer and looked down at the poster. Bright red with startling black writing, it displayed a large picture of Max and the announcement Max Arragen, Wanted, Dead or Alive!!!

CHAPTER FOUR

THE silence in the room was electric. All three seemed frozen in place. Finally, Kayla looked up at Max and asked simply, "What does it mean?"

He didn't meet her gaze. "I have no idea," he said softly, still staring at the poster. His mind was working like a buzz saw, cutting through all options and leaving shards of rejected possibilities behind. What could he possibly have done…?

Pellea crossed her arms over her chest and glared at him. "Okay, if nothing comes quickly to mind, let's go over the facts. As you can see, this was issued by the small nation of Mercuria. Have you ever been there?"

He raised his head and looked at the queen. This was a can of worms he would rather not have to deal with, but it seemed he would have no choice.

"Yes. I've been there."

"When? What were you doing there?"

Kayla was glaring at him now, as well. Interesting that they both seemed to assume he must be guilty of something. But then, he probably deserved that. If he didn't want people to suspect shenanigans, he should have lived a different sort of life. Was it too late to change? Probably. He frowned.

"I spent a few months there last year. I did some work for the government. Actually, I helped them set up their air force."

Pellea's eyebrows rose at that. "And then what happened?"

He thought about it for a moment. Funny how things that seemed so mundane at the time became so impossible to explain to anyone. This looked a little more serious than he'd expected. But try as he might, he couldn't remember having done anything illegal while he was there. He hadn't robbed anyone. He hadn't run off with the royal jewels. He hadn't stolen any plans. The only thing he could think of that might apply had been a broken relationship with a rather beautiful... Well, he wasn't going to tell these ladies about that. They wouldn't be happy to hear it. And anyway that had been over a year ago.

He faced them squarely and tried to look candid. "I have to think it over and see if I can figure out what they are actually talking about."

"You can't tell us now?" Kayla asked.

He looked at her and shook his head. "No. I'm sorry. You're going to have to wait until I get a bit clearer on just exactly what they're objecting to."

Kayla and Pellea were both staring at him with wide-eyed wonder. Both sets of eyes contained the same horrified expression. It was pretty clear that they both thought that anything that couldn't be explained right here, right now, in simple language, had to be pretty darn bad. He looked at them both and shrugged, hating to feel defensive this way. Why should he have to explain himself?

But he was trapped. Sooner or later, they would probably know everything about his life—even things he didn't know. Still, why make it easy for them?

"I haven't led a perfect life. I've done things I'm not proud of. Things I wouldn't want to tell you about."

Pellea nodded as though she'd thought as much, but Kayla appeared surprised and troubled. He regretted that. But he still wasn't going to tell her everything he'd ever done wrong in his life. He wasn't going to tell anyone.

"I'm sorry," he said simply. "But I'm going to find out what they are accusing me of before I start spilling my guts and go admitting to every crime known to have happened in the last ten years. You understand?"

He looked at them. They looked back, and it was clear they didn't understand. It was obvious neither one of them had ever done anything to be ashamed of in their lives. Or not much, anyway. They stared at him with huge eyes and didn't say a thing. He groaned.

Suddenly, he was a little angry. "You know what? I didn't ask for this gig. I don't know much yet about what it means to be a prince. And I'm starting to feel like it's going to crowd me a bit. I live my life pretty free and easy." He shook his head, looking from one to the other of them. "I don't know, maybe that sort of living is incompatible with royal structure. What do you think?"

They just stared and he began to feel uncomfortable. In his experience, women talked over everything. They never quit. What was with the silent treatment? Did they really think he'd done something so awful it couldn't be talked about at all?

He was about to ask about that when Pellea made a move toward him. As he watched, she walked up and grabbed him by the front of his shirt, pulling his face down inches from hers.

"Promise me you won't run away," she said fiercely.

That was a tough one. "Um…for how long?"

There was a pause while she seemed to digest his attitude and realize he was close to an edge she didn't want to reach. She closed her eyes for a second, then opened them again. "Promise me you will give this a month."

A month. Could he take a month of this constant royal oversight?

He shook his head. "How can I do that?" he said, his tone almost sarcastic. "I may have to go serve time in East Slobovia here." He gestured toward the poster, then pulled back and used his most disarming smile. "How about a week?"

She winced and made a concession to reality. "Two weeks."

He glanced at Kayla. She looked like she was holding her breath. He drew in a long breath himself and nodded as he looked back at the queen.

"Okay. I can give you that."

She let go and gave him a pat where she'd been grabbing his shirt. "Come to me tomorrow and be ready to tell me everything," she said as she headed for the door.

"I'll tell you what I feel you need to know," he countered as she opened it.

She whirled and glared at him. "Listen, Max. I hope you understand that you must take this seriously. So far, I've been able to keep this nonsense out of the king's notice. But if things get more dicey, I'm going to have to go to him with it."

Kayla bit her lip, wanting to stop Pellea. Didn't she see how he resented being talked to like this? Didn't she notice the sarcastic twist to the corner of his mouth, the veiled anger in his deep blue eyes?

She was actually surprised he hadn't said anything. He was used to talking back and walking out. It wasn't going to be easy for him to learn to hold his tongue and take honest criticism. Was he going to be able to handle it?

"Tomorrow," Pellea said. "And you will tell me all."

"Or at least as much of it as I know myself."

She threw back an exasperated look, but this time she didn't stop. In a few seconds, the door was closing and he and Kayla were alone again.

She turned to him, her eyes huge and dark in the lamplight.

"Max, what did you do?"

He took a deep breath and faced her. This was almost funny. Maybe someday they would look back and laugh. But not today.

"You know what? I don't have a clue." He saw the skepticism in her eyes and he looked away, swearing softly. "I've done a lot of things, Kayla. Nothing ever seemed bad enough to deserve jail time. Or death." He turned back and looked at her. "But you never know. People take things more seriously than you think at the time."

She shook her head slowly, almost in wonder. "Mercuria. It's a simple little country. You never even think of it. It's smaller than Ambria. What can they be so upset about?"

He shrugged, a little annoyed that no one seemed to have any faith in him. But he knew that wasn't fair. He'd given no one any reason to trust him. When you lived on the edge of a knife blade, like he had, you had to know that people were going to back away in horror now and then. It came with the territory.

"I'd have to see more than a picture on a Wanted poster to know that for sure."

He gave her a long, slow look, then shrugged again and headed for the door.

"I'd like to see a full description of my crime," he said, managing to sound lighthearted and carefree again. Free and easy. That was the way he wanted to live. "You've got to see what you're charged with before you can mount any sort of defense. Basic legal advice."

He turned and gave her a wink, then made it out the door and into the castle hallways.

Kayla watched the door swing shut and she drew air deep into her lungs. Secrets. He had secrets.

Well, funny thing. So did she.

The following morning when she got to work, Kayla found the queen involved in a dispute between a kitchen prep assistant and the royal chef. She was claiming the older man had promised to advance her and now he seemed to be spending all his time giving extra training to the pretty new pastry chef.

"Who knew my fabulously exciting days as queen would be filled with this sort of relationship management?" she complained to Kayla. "I might as well be working for the local department store." She sighed. "But I do feel sorry for her. He has been leading her on."

"Call the chef in for a nice chat, tell him that his grilled rosemary scallops are to-die-for and mention that reports of favoritism will be noted on his permanent record," Kayla advised. "And just to be safe, make sure he knows canoodling in the broom closet will be frowned upon."

Pellea shook her head. "You see it all so clearly, my dear. I know exactly why I hired you."

Kayla gave her a quizzical smile. "No regrets?"

Pellea pursed her lips and slid down into the chair opposite from where Kayla sat at her desk. "Okay. Let's get into it." She fixed her with a steady look. "Do I have anything to worry about?"

Kayla managed to look completely innocent. "In what way?"

Pellea gave her a look. "I think you know what I'm talking about. I have plans for Max, so it would be best if we put all our cards on the table, don't you agree?" She thought of something and her eyes narrowed. "By the way, where was your baby last night? I didn't see any evidence that he was with you."

Kayla's heart began to beat a bit harder. "He was nearby. He was staying down the hall with my sister."

"Oh." Pellea still looked skeptical.

Kayla leaned forward earnestly, determined not to let Pellea go down the road she obviously had been moving toward.

"No, it's not like that. Teddy often stays with Caroline when I work late. She watches him during the day, and her little one is the same age. He was already asleep…"

She stopped, realizing she was giving too much information. That was always the perfect way to sound absolutely guilty as charged. Taking a deep breath, she added simply, "I had no idea that Max was going to drop by."

Pellea blinked rapidly. "Just how close were you and Max in the old days?"

"We were good friends. Very good friends." She sighed and looked directly into the queen's eyes. "What you saw when you came in was a result of us both remembering Eddie and comforting each other over losing him that way."

Pellea held her gaze steady and slightly shook her head. "It looked like more than that to me."

Her heart rate made another lurch. "Pellea, I adored my husband," she said forcefully. "He was my life." She shook her head, hair flying about her shoulders. "Max loved him, too. Everybody did. He was a wonderful man." Reaching out, she took Pellea's hands in hers. "Please understand. Max and I were never…"

She stopped short, turning red. She couldn't really say that, could she? To her horror, she realized it was a lie. And she couldn't lie to Pellea of all people. She stared, wide-eyed, not sure how to get out of this trap she'd wandered into.

But Pellea didn't seem to notice. She nodded, searching her eyes with a sense of sympathy and compassion that didn't leave any more room for suspicion. "Okay. Oh, Kayla, I understand, and I'm sorry if it seemed I was implying anything more." She smiled with a sweetness that had once been her trademark, but wasn't often seen of late. "I won't do it again."

"Thanks." She smiled back, feeling a sense of relief that her friend and employer cared enough to make that pledge. And yet, in the pit of her stomach there lurked an aching tangle of guilt.

As of now, it seemed she was the only one who remembered what had happened that last night in Trialta. She had to keep it that way. But how could she do that when temptation was always lurking?

Somehow, she had to work at distancing herself from Max. She had to be unavailable when he was around. It shouldn't be too hard. He was going to be very busy getting to know the rest of the royals and learning what his duties and responsibilities would be here in the castle. She would try to stay just as busy somewhere else. She might even ask for another assignment on the continent, one where she could take Teddy with her.

Yes, that was a good idea. She would leave the castle for a while. She would do something. She had to fix this. And she would.

"Did he tell you why Mercuria wants him to come back and stand trial?" Pellea asked.

"No. He didn't seem to know why."

"Hmmph." Pellea didn't sound convinced. "It's a real problem, you know. We owe that country a lot. They helped us during the war. Without their help, we might not have succeeded. And now that we've got a sort of truce going, they are the ones who act as go-between, our line of communication to the Granvillis. They're strong allies. I can't turn my back on a solid request like this. I can't ignore our friends. They won't be there for us next time if I do."

The worry in her voice sent Kayla's nerves quivering. They couldn't possibly be considering giving him up to the Mercurian royals—could they? Impossible.

"Send out the diplomats," she suggested, only half joking.

"Oh, definitely. Droves of them." She smiled, but it faded quickly. "I've got to admit, it worries me quite a bit. I'm going to have to make a call to them soon. I've got to tell them something. Max is going to have to level with me. And regardless, we'll have to find some way to either meet their demands or placate them."

"Meet their demands?" Kayla repeated, her dread growing.

Pellea gave her a reassuring pat. "Placating is probably safer," she noted. Then she made a face. "If we sent him back to them, lord only knows what he might do."

Kayla was beginning to rebel. After all, he wasn't all that bad. A bit nonconformist, of course, but all in all, he was definitely a good guy, at least in her experience with him.

But Pellea was still thinking of examples. She shook her head. "Last night at the ball, when he was presented to the old duchess, my Great-Aunt Judis, I was afraid he was going to say something like, 'Hey, Toots, could you get me a refill on this drink while you're up?'"

Kayla's eyes widened. "He didn't!"

"No, he didn't." She raised a significant eyebrow. "But there's something about him that keeps making me scared he will."

Despite her regard for him as a man, Kayla knew exactly what she meant. She frowned, trying to key in to the heart of the matter.

"He just doesn't have the proper instincts."

"Exactly."

She looked up hopefully. "He'll learn."

Pellea sighed. "Of course he will. But can we wait around for that to develop on its own? I think not." She drew in a deep breath. "So I'm getting him a superior teacher."

"Really?" Kayla's heart fell but she fought against it. This was just what had to happen. He had to learn his place in the scheme of things and she had to keep her distance from the entire process. It was all for the best and she knew it. "Who is that?"

Pellea stared at her, lips pursed as though she were annoyed with her somehow.

"A wonderful woman. She's perfect for this assignment. Her only flaw is that she is rather slow on the uptake at times." She gave a sound of exasperation. "It's someone he already respects and has a great affection for."

"Really?" She was still frowning. She hadn't realized he knew that many women here. But what was she thinking? He always knew women, wherever he happened to be. "Do I know her?"

Pellea threw up her hands. "It's you, silly. And you have exactly one week to perform a magical transformation."

Max arrived at Pellea's office in a somewhat surly mood. He'd spent the morning thinking about what he was going to say to her and nothing very good had come to mind. He decided to go for the basics—to tell her why he'd been in Mercuria and how his work there went. Then maybe she could weave some sort of conspiracy out of it all.

"Good morning, Your Majesty," he said cheerfully as she rose to greet him. He kissed both cheeks and smiled at her.

"You just missed Kayla," she told him. "I sent her on an errand." She gave him a sharp look. "But that will give us a chance to talk openly, won't it?"

He frowned, not sure he appreciated her implications that there might be things he could tell her that he wouldn't tell Kayla. Still, he followed her lead and sat across from her at her desk.

"I take it you have something to tell me?" she said, looking almost eager.

He shrugged and took a deep breath. "I've made some inquiries. I've got a few ideas."

"Good. Tell me what they are, because I don't have a clue."

He chewed on his lower lip, then admitted evasively, "I don't really have anything definitive."

She looked disappointed. "You don't know why the Mercurians are angry with you?"

He laughed shortly. "Angry, sure. Ready to lock me away in a dungeon...not so much."

Pellea's eyes were cooler now. "Why don't we start at the beginning?" she suggested. "Maybe there's something you're just not noticing. Why don't you tell me everything? All about your time in Mercuria."

He felt his jaw tighten, but he knew he really couldn't blame her. So he tried to do it her way.

"Okay. It all started when an old flight instructor of mine recommended me to the

Mercurian Army as someone who might be able to help them get an air force organized and trained. I flew over, met the king and talked to the military people in charge. It seemed like a decent little country, trying to emerge onto the global stage, but without a lot of money and mainly ancient aircraft at their disposal. The jets were going to have to come later. Anyway, I thought I could help them. Why not? So I signed on."

"How long were you there?"

"Not quite a year."

She nodded, thinking about what he'd told her and frowning. "Were you successful?"

"I thought so. We got a good skeleton of a program started."

She nodded again. "Did you know they were helping us with our war effort?"

"Of course. That was one reason the project appealed to me. I'm Ambrian, too."

"Why did you leave?"

That was a harder question. There were too many threads making up that answer to get into right now.

"Actually, around that time some old flying friends of mine showed up and talked me into coming over to join the fight for the restoration of the monarchy here in Ambria. It sounded like fun. Aerial combat and all that. And I was growing tired of all the bureaucracy I had to deal with in Mercuria. I wanted to get back into real flying again. So I joined up." He looked at her expectantly, his story over.

She sighed, shaking her head. "Which tells me a lot," she muttered, "and nothing."

"Exactly."

She studied his face for a moment. "Were they angry that you left when you did? Did they feel you hadn't completed your commitment?"

He shook his head. "There might have been a little of that, but no one actually complained. They knew I was ready to go."

He leaned forward. She deserved a better answer, but he just didn't know what he could tell her that was going to give her the information she needed.

"Pellea, I did a lot of things that someone might look back on and decide were… out of bounds, perhaps. We were flyers. We raised hell. That's what we do."

Slowly, she shook her head. "I'm pretty sure this is more than raising hell," she said. "You don't say 'dead or alive' about a little carousing."

"Okay, maybe…maybe an old girlfriend decided to take some sort of revenge. Maybe an innkeeper decided to blame me for a fight that might have torn up his bar and is suing for damages. Maybe someone who felt slighted by me in some way wants a pound of flesh. I just don't know. And I'm not sure what you want me to do about it." He shrugged. "Do you want me to issue an apology?"

"What? No. Of course not. Not until we know just what this is about."

He bit his tongue, wishing he could lose the defensive attitude. He knew he hadn't been living an exemplary life. He regretted it. Talking with Pellea, he wasn't proud of it. But it was lousy being asked to explain it. Life was complicated enough without this stupid wanted poster arriving from Mercuria.

He sat back. "Leave it to me. I think I can handle this. It might take a little time, but I'll get in touch with people I knew when I was there. I'll let you know for sure when I think I've really got it pinned down."

She nodded slowly. "Do that," she said. "But make it soon."

Kayla knew Max was going in to see Pellea first thing and she hoped they would be able to settle matters. It might be better if she could be there to help things along, but she had some business on the other side of the castle and knew she would probably miss him. So she left Max a message to meet her in the hall of portraits, and to her surprise, he was right on time.

The fact that there *was* a hall of portraits was a miracle. During the original rebellion, when the Granvillis had burned most of the castle and killed the king and queen—the parents of the current crop of princes, as well as of King Monte, Pellea's husband—they had destroyed everything they could get their hands on that might remind anyone of the deposed monarchy. A lot of paintings burned that night, but many of the most important ones were spirited out by various servants who hid them with relatives for the twenty-five years of the Granvilli regime.

After the restoration of the DeAngelis monarchy, when the castle archivist began to collect them and bring them home, there was a wave of emotion in the populace that touched them all. It was so very important to have these beautiful pictures to tell the story of what their history had been.

Kayla found Max gazing up at a huge stately portrait of his great grandfather. The fine-looking royal was wearing an ermine-lined cape and looking quite imperial and majestic.

"Quite a handsome bunch, your ancestors," she noted, sliding in beside him and looking up as well. She felt proud for him, proud for Ambria. She only hoped he understood what it meant to be a part of this.

"They certainly seem well-turned out," he agreed. "But then, you've always got artistic flattery on your side when you're royalty." He gave her a mock jab in the ribs with his elbow. "The artist makes them beautiful or he doesn't get paid, I would think."

"Maybe." She gave him a sideways look.

"But from the evidence presented by your brothers, I'd chock it all up to good genes."

He shrugged and she frowned, not sure he was sufficiently impressed.

"After all, the blood of these very people flows in your veins," she pointed out.

He grunted. "Let's hope none of them were bleeders or vampires," he said lightly. "Don't those two things tend to run in this kind of family?"

For some reason him saying that made her absolutely furious. Did he really not understand how important his own family was? Or was he just trying to drive her crazy?

"There is no such thing as vampires," she said through clenched teeth.

"Maybe not," he said, his blue eyes sparkling with amusement. "But I'm going to start being more careful with the morning shave. You never know."

"No one in the DeAngelis family has ever shown any signs of hemophilia," she protested, trying hard not to let him see how annoyed she was. "Just forget it."

He gave her a look that infuriated her even further, then shrugged again and turned away as though it hardly affected him anyway. She took a deep breath and forced herself to calm down. She knew she was being overly sensitive, and that he was playing on her emotions like a skilled musician. She had to hold it back. She couldn't give him the satisfaction of showing her feelings like this.

Slowly, she followed as he examined one portrait after another. She'd been here often in the last few months and she didn't have to look at the labels to know who each one was. She was ready to answer any of his questions, but he didn't say another word and she wondered what he was thinking.

No matter what, he had to be fascinated by the imposing DeAngelis family. Who could help it? And to think that he'd suddenly found out he was one of them.

They'd walked the length of the hall and then they both went out onto the terrace that overlooked the royal fields. Leaning against the massive stone guardrail, he smiled at her and her annoyance with his attitude began to melt away. She really couldn't resist that smile.

"Did you talk to Pellea?" she asked.

"Oh, yeah. We had a little chat."

"And?"

He eyed her questioningly. "What? You think I'm going to tell you everything I told her?"

She pulled back quickly. "No. Of course not."

He laughed and reached out to push her hair behind her ear and then pull her closer again. "But you know I would. If there was anything to tell."

"You didn't come up with anything?" Her skin tingled where his fingers had touched and she frowned, trying to ignore it.

He hesitated. "Not anything sure. Or substantive." He shrugged and changed the subject. "I can't get over you being here like this," he said. "What are the odds that we would both end up in the Ambrian castle? That was certainly a stroke of luck."

"Yes, wasn't it?"

She looked at his beautiful eyes and the hard, tanned planes of his handsome face and she knew he belonged with the men and women in those huge, gorgeously painted portraits in the hall. Someday his image would hang there with them. That was his destiny. Surely he knew that. Didn't he?

"So how did Pellea find you, anyway?" he was asking her. "You said your sister had something to do with it?"

"I told you we'd known each other before. When my sister and her husband moved here, Caroline went to Pellea and told her about me and my situation and let her know I was looking for a job. It just so happened that she was looking for an assistant. So everything fell into place."

"Good timing. Life can happen that way sometimes."

She nodded ruefully. "Not often."

"No." A shadow flickered through his gaze. "Not often."

They stood silently for a moment, each thinking private thoughts. Kayla was remembering Eddie and she was pretty sure he was, too. But she didn't want to get started on that again. They had work to do.

"I guess you're wondering why I asked you to meet me here," she said at last.

He grinned at her using such a well-known cliché. "The question had crossed my mind a time or two," he admitted. "And then I decided you just wanted me to learn to connect with my roots."

"A simple goal, I would think."

He grimaced. "So okay, I looked each ancient ancestor in the eye and took his measure. And the women, too. And I was impressed." But he seemed a little impatient. "What else do you want from me?"

She drew a deep breath in slowly, wondering how to put this. She had no idea how he was going to take it. For all she knew, he might storm off and never speak to her again. Finally, she just blurted it out.

"Okay, Max. Here's the deal." She steeled herself. "Pellea wants me to teach you how to act like a prince."

CHAPTER FIVE

MAX stared at her and for a moment, Kayla thought he hadn't understood. But a faint smile quirked at the corners of his mouth and he repeated slowly, "Pellea wants you to teach me how to act like a prince?"

She nodded, waiting.

He gave her a look as though this was about as kooky as he'd thought things could get. "Really?" he said with a twist to his smile. "Who taught you?"

That was a good question and keyed right in to her deepest fears about this assignment. But she wasn't going to let him know that. She hadn't asked for this. In fact, she wished it hadn't occurred to Pellea at all. But it had, and here they were, stuck with a project to do.

"I'm very observant," she said cheekily. "Don't worry. I won't steer you wrong."

He grinned, watching her with a slightly lascivious expression. "I'm not worried at all. I have every intention of becoming teacher's pet in a major way."

She pretended to frown. "Don't count on that, mister. I'm a tough grader. You're going to have to earn your graduation papers."

"It's a deal." He pretended to look at his watch. "You've got two weeks to make me into royalty. Better get moving."

She wasn't crazy about the way he set it up like an adversarial position, but she'd known from the start that she would have to work fast. He didn't have to remind her. His attention span wouldn't last long. And he proved it by jumping to a new topic in seconds.

A man had walked by holding a baby, and they both looked up as the baby made a cooing sound. She met Max's wide eyes and they both smiled.

"Hey, when do I get to meet little… Teddy, did you say his name was?" he asked.

She felt a surge of unpleasant adrenaline. "Yes, uh…Teddy."

He looked at her curiously. "Is he here at the castle with you?"

"He stays with my sister during the day. I'll…uh…make sure you get to meet him soon."

"Good." He frowned and she knew he was wondering why she was so hesitant. "I'll bet he looks just like Eddie."

Color filled her cheeks. She tried to force it back but it just kept coming. Had he noticed? Did he see how uncomfortable she was with this?

"He's a little young to look like anyone right now," she said breathlessly.

But he didn't seem to notice her reaction. He was looking into the past, his brows pulled together, and thinking of how it had once been. "Thank God you had his baby," he said softly, reaching out to touch her cheek. "Thank God there's a piece of him left in the world."

Her mind was racing. She had to think of something. Hopefully, he would forget about Teddy once he was thoroughly invested in taking on the royal mantle. That had to be her goal: to convince him that becoming a prince was something he wanted to do, that it would engage his mind and spirit like nothing else he'd ever done. Once he opened himself to it fully, he would be so busy, so connected with what was going on here in the castle, that he would forget about her and her son. They would just fade into a pleasant memory for him, and then her life could go on as it had before he ever got here.

But he was still frowning at her, searching her eyes. She pulled away from his hand and turned to look at the distant sea. They were miles away, but she thought she could hear the waves pounding on the rocks.

"Listen, what about this Mercuria situation? I know you don't know exactly what their beef is, but you must have some idea of what set them off." She turned back to look at him. "Any clue at all as to what their problem was?"

He stared at her for a moment, then gave a bitter laugh. "You mean why they want to lock me away in their particularly nasty tower and torture me with bad food? No. I'm still not sure what that is all about."

She frowned. "Come on, Max. You must have a secret opinion. Or two."

"Oh, yeah. I've got some thoughts on the matter." He frowned and shifted his weight from one foot to the other, as though suddenly uncomfortable with those very thoughts. "But you wouldn't like them."

That gave her a momentary pang, but she was game. "Try me."

He made a face. "I'd rather not."

She looked into his eyes. He was serious.

"Max, this isn't a game. We have to find out the truth. This has to be dealt with."

He nodded slowly. "Of course."

She waited. He stood very still and watched her. She sighed with quick exasperation and tugged on his sleeve. "Max! Tell me! Delve down into your deepest intuitions and tell me what you think it just might be."

He grimaced, then looked back at her and shrugged. "Okay. If you really want me to do this, here you go. This is just a guess, but..." He took a deep breath, then looked out at the distant mountains. "I think they want me to marry their princess."

She stared at him in shock. He glanced at her and sighed.

"And here you thought this was the only royal gig I had lined up," he said grimly. "But no. I've got my choice. Lucky me."

Kayla swallowed hard. She hadn't expected something like this. Staring at Max, she tried to get her mind around these new developments. Everything inside her was aching for a denial. He couldn't…could he? He hadn't…had he?

"Is there…uh…a reason they would be demanding this? I mean, their charges were pretty hard-line, even if they weren't explicit."

His blue gaze skimmed her features. "You mean, did I compromise the girl's reputation in some way?" he said with a trace of sarcasm and a touch of resentment. "No, Kayla. I did not."

"Oh." Relief flooded her, leaving her breathless. And then she realized she still didn't know any of the details. "Then…?"

"The Princess Nadine is fifteen years old," he told her, looking almost angry. "She decided to get a teenage crush on me. I didn't do a thing to encourage it. Believe me, I do have certain scruples. But girls that age…" He shrugged and looked toward the heavens for help.

It was ridiculous. Maddening. And ultimately, he had a feeling it would be quite embarrassing. There had to be a way to handle this without everyone knowing what the Mercurians really wanted.

Princess Nadine was a lovely girl, but she was much too young to be handed off to an old guy like him. He'd only seen her a few times and he'd managed to keep those visits short. He couldn't go back there. There was no telling what would be demanded of him. The family running the country was a few bricks short of a load at times. One might even say, crazy as loons.

"It's not a good situation."

"Oh."

"She decided she wanted me. And her daddy, the King of Mercuria, gives her whatever she wants."

"Oh, dear."

"Yes. 'Oh, dear'." He finally looked her in the eye. "So how am I supposed to explain this to Pellea? Especially when I don't even know if it's true?"

She thought for a moment. It was a problem. The queen was not going to be happy, and this put her in an awkward position in regard to an international relations situation that would just tangle things into knots. She could see why he hesitated to tell her about it.

But he would have to.

"You haven't said anything to her about this?"

"No."

She nodded. "Explain it to her just like you did to me."

He looked skeptical. "I don't think she'll buy it."

"If it's the truth, what else can you do?"

He gave her a baleful look and shook his head. "Run away?" he suggested, only half joking.

"Never," she said firmly.

He looked weary. "You know, this is just a guess. I don't have any evidence. I'm not sure this is the exact thing pulling their chain. For all I know..."

"You've got to tell her. Right now."

"Right now? But..."

She dug for her mobile and held up a

hand to stop him. "I'll see if she's in," she said, punching in Pellea's office number. "She's not there," she said after a moment. "But her message says she'll be right back."

Leaning on the stone guard wall, he was watching her from under dark, lowered lashes. "You're bound and determined to make sure I do the right thing, aren't you? And by that, I mean the 'royal' right thing." His eyes narrowed further. "You remind me of a prison warden I once knew."

She looked up at him, doggedly set in her goals. "I'm going to make you into a prince," she said coolly. "And you're going to like it."

He didn't smile. His blue eyes looked as cold and hard as sapphire stones. "Or else I'll bow out," he said softly.

Holding his gaze, she shook her head slowly. "Over my dead body," she promised, enunciating each word carefully. "You're sticking this out, mister."

He stared a moment longer, and then his lip began to curl. "Damn," he said huskily. "Do you know how sexy you look when you're giving me orders?"

"Oh!" She turned and started away,

furious with him again. Was he ever going to take anything seriously?

"Hey." He caught up with her and grabbed her upper arm, pulling her around to face him. "I'm sorry. I'm sure you thought that was condescending, didn't you? I didn't mean it that way. I was just being honest."

She glared at him. "Be honest with Pellea. She's the one who counts. And believe me, she's ready to give you every chance in the world. But you have to level with her. Come on." She linked her arm with his and gazed up at him, intense and a bit anxious. "Let's go on over to the office. She ought to be back any minute. And you can tell her yourself. She'll listen."

He gave her a skeptical look. "She'll try to see my side of things?"

"Oh, absolutely. She's really very understanding."

"I really don't understand any of this and what's more, I won't have it!"

Kayla recoiled. She'd never seen Pellea so angry. She glanced apologetically at Max, but he was scowling at the queen.

Oh, brother, did she ever regret forcing this little conversation.

They had come back to the office and found Pellea just arriving, a sheaf of papers in her hand. Obviously, she'd had news. She'd greeted them both the way someone thoroughly annoyed might, and as things were going, that did seem to be exactly what she was.

Pellea took a deep breath, closed her eyes and tried to calm herself. "All right. I'm going to try not to shout. That sort of thing is never becoming in a queen." She gestured at them, slipping into her desk chair. "Sit down. We'll do this the right way." But her eyes flashed at Max. "Now tell me again, what exactly have you heard from Mercuria?"

Every muscle he owned seemed to be locked in stone. "As I said before, not much."

There was a hard line to his mouth that Kayla didn't like. She knew he resented being talked to the way Pellea had done, but she could also see that he was holding back. She only prayed that he was in control of his emotions. And that Pellea was, too. Sinking into a chair, she tugged on his sleeve to get him to sit down, too.

"I do have some calls in to some people and a friend is trying to look into this further, but…" He shrugged. "So far, not much."

"You're right," Pellea said evenly. "That's not much." She waved an official-looking document at him. "I'll tell you what I have. We've just received it. It's from their foreign minister." Her eyes blazed.

Max's head went back defensively and his eyes were hooded. "What does he have to say?"

She rattled the paper. "He says we have five days to the deadline and at that point, they expect us to hand you over."

A muscle pulsed at his jawline. "And if you don't hand me over?"

She glared at him. "They're going to invade."

Kayla gasped. "What? Oh, Pellea, that can't be."

The queen looked at Kayla, at a loss and showing it. "That's what they say, right here." She held up the embossed announcement, complete with signatures and an official stamp. "Read it and weep."

"They won't invade," Max scoffed. "They don't have the man power." But he perused the document carefully, reading every line.

Pellea seemed to be counting to ten. Finally, she said a bit breathlessly, "Maybe they won't actually invade. Maybe this is all bluster. But that doesn't fix everything. We still owe this country a lot. We need to pay them back, in kind if not in cash. What are we going to do to satisfy them? What are we going to do about their demand to have you extradited?"

His gaze was steady and firm. "We're going to tell them to pound sand, I hope."

"No." She shook her head emphatically.

His face registered a tiny flash of shock, then one eyebrow rose quizzically. "You want me to go and stand trial?" he asked incredulously.

"Of course not. But we don't get around it by yelling at them." She threw her hands up. "We consult. We sympathize. We question. We find ways to talk them out of their anger. We don't give them exactly what they want, but we make them think we did."

Max frowned, not sure he bought her song and dance. "But we still don't know exactly what they want from me."

"No. We don't, do we?" Pellea tapped the toe of her shoe against the tiled floor and stared at him steadily. "The only one here who could possibly know is you. So what do you think it is? If you were to venture a guess."

Max stared back. Kayla waited breathlessly, expecting him to find a way to tell the queen about the princess, just the way he'd told her. She waited. And waited.

But Max didn't say a word about that. Instead, his handsome face seemed to have cleansed itself of all emotion, all thought, and he said evenly, "I think you already have a theory. Don't you? Why don't you tell me what it is?"

"A theory? No." She pulled another large sheet of paper off her desk and brandished it. "But the foreign minister of Mercuria seems to have one. Here's what he says." She held it up and began to read, just skimming to the pertinent words and phrases.

"According to the foreign minister, while you were in their lovely country, enjoying their delightful hospitality…" She took a deep breath before going on, setting up a nicely dramatic pause. "You stole a horse, hijacked an airplane and made off with an important ancient historical national artifact." She lowered the paper and looked him in the eye. "And you say…?"

He was shaking his head, half laughing, but without amusement. "That's insane. I never took any artifact."

Kayla groaned and Pellea's eyes widened. "But the horse and the airplane…?"

He grimaced. This was all so stupid. "Listen, I can explain."

Pellea looked at Kayla. Kayla looked at Pellea. They both groaned.

"No, really," he said, feeling unfairly outnumbered. "There was no money in the treasury. They gave me the plane in lieu of payment for services rendered. I can prove it."

Pellea's eyes flashed. "Good. You'll have to. Do you have papers?"

He hesitated and then he shrugged. "I'll

have to take a look. I must have something somewhere."

She nodded as though she'd known that all along. "And the horse?"

He drew in a long breath. "That's a longer story."

"Of course." She was glaring again. "And the artifact?"

His eyes blazed at that one. "Now there, I have no idea what they're talking about."

Pellea's eyes narrowed. "Oh, but I think you do."

"Do you?" His back was really up now. "Then why don't you tell me?"

She searched his eyes for a moment, then shrugged. "We're going to put together a letter of explanation," she said, completely dismissing the subject of the artifact for now, "and send an ambassador right away."

"For this?" he said dismissively.

She turned and looked at him. "Don't you understand how important this is? We have to soothe ruffled feathers as quickly as we can." Her eyes flashed and her hands smoothed down the bright red dress she was wearing, the outfit that was making her look like a Spanish dancer. "Unless you'd like to go back and explain it to them yourself?"

He winced. "I don't think that would be a good idea."

"Just so," she said, as though that proved some point she'd been making all along.

Watching all this, Kayla was at a loss. She knew Max was being cagey. Why hadn't he brought up the princess? Why did he treat Pellea like someone he had to keep things from? She wished he would lay it all out for her. If they didn't handle this properly, war could be the result.

Either that, or extradition. She shuddered.

"Pellea, does Monte...does the king know about this?" she asked her.

"No." Her face crumpled and for a second, Kayla was afraid she would cry. But she regained her composure quickly, taking Kayla's hand in hers and squeezing it as though grateful she had her support and understanding. "No, he's got his own international relations problems right now. I don't want to bother him with this. I have to begin taking care of these things on my own and not go running to him with everything."

Kayla nodded sympathetically. Working with Pellea, she had seen for herself what a precarious tightrope she walked trying to become effective without becoming either obsessive or too dependent. She and Monte had been like the perfect couple from the beginning, in more ways than one. Their royal marriage was a partnership and Pellea worked at it night and day.

Max rose, looking moody. "Your Majesty, let me just say this. The list you received from the foreign minister sounds like a bunch of excuses to me. I don't know what's really behind all this." He stopped and swallowed hard. It really wasn't easy for him to delve into his life and try to find explanations for this. But he would try.

"Why not wait until I find out something from my contacts in the country. Just hold on until then. Maybe we'll have something we can work with."

Pellea nodded, looking distracted. "Of course. You'll let me know, won't you?" She waved them off. "Until then, I'll be counting on Kayla to manage things. So

go, both of you. Get some lunch. I'll talk
to you later."

Kayla looked back as they closed the
door. A jagged little piece of her heart tore
at the look in Pellea's face. She bit her lip
and turned away.

They walked away from the office. Kayla
eyed at Max sideways and wondered how
to broach the subject that was begging to
be discussed. She kept expecting all this
to be cleared up, and instead, she was just
getting more confused.

"You want to explain all that to me?" she
said at last, when he didn't volunteer anything.

He looked down at her and raised an
eyebrow. "You mean, why I didn't tell her
about Princess Nadine?"

She nodded. "You could start with that."

He shrugged and kept walking. "There
was nothing about it in the complaint. So
maybe I'm wrong. Maybe that's not what
this is all about."

She stopped him and searched his eyes
in wonder. "You don't believe that."

He glanced back at her, frowning. "Who

cares what I believe, Kayla. What does it matter?"

"Of course what you believe matters. How are we going to get to the bottom of all this if we just throw out theories without exploring them?"

She saw the torture in his eyes and melted. "Listen." She grabbed his arm and pressed close so she could talk to him softly. "Whatever they think you did, whatever it turns out to be, we'll handle it. Nothing is going to drive you away. We won't let it." His gaze locked in hers. "I won't let it," she whispered, her love for him in her eyes.

He reached up and his hand cupped her chin, fingers trailing across her cheek. He didn't say a word, but something in his eyes said volumes. *I need you, Kayla,* they seemed to be saying. *Don't ever leave me. I don't want to live without you. Never again.*

She saw it as clearly as though he had said the words aloud. But she also saw what followed—a regret, a denial. She'd seen his true feelings, but at the same time, she saw why he couldn't act on them. It was all there. As Pellea had said, read them and weep.

He dropped his hand and looked away and she put distance between them and cleared her throat.

"Tell me about the horse," she said coolly.

Something flashed in his eyes and he turned away, then steeled himself and turned back and said, "Let's get some food first. Where's the closest place to get some food around here?"

She led him there and they entered the fast-food cavalcade, all chrome and neon flashing lights, with simple tables and chairs and a counter for ordering your food. Colors screamed from all sides and music was loud and aggressive. He scanned the place, then looked down at her and shook his head, his eyes amused.

"Are you going to tell me this is one of your favorite places?" he said skeptically.

She raised her chin and tried to keep from smiling, though his gorgeous eyes were tempting her to laugh. "Hey, I hang out here all the time." She glanced around the room while he grinned at her obvious lie. "And anyway, you asked for something close."

He bit his lower lip and attempted to adjust the criteria. "How about the closest decent food where you can also hear yourself think?"

"Say no more," she said and led him to the escalator, then around two corners and onto a quieter walkway. "How about this?"

She would have thought the Two for Tea tearoom might have been a little too precious for his taste, but he smiled and nodded. "Looks great," he said.

She grinned. "I hadn't figured you for finger sandwiches," she said.

"That shows how little you really know me," he replied, and escorted her in.

Every table had a lace cloth. The tea was served in fragile cups and saucers and the trays of scones and little sandwiches were passed from table to table by girls in Victorian costumes. Music by Debussy, Liszt and Chopin filled the air. Kayla sighed. Just what they needed to calm the frantic mood of the day.

They sat, ordered and then smiled at each other across the table.

"We came here to talk," she reminded him.

He made a face. "Yes." He sighed. "What was the subject again?"

"The horse."

"Ah, yes. The horse." His eyes widened, full of innocence. "Okay, I did steal the horse."

She gasped. "What? I thought you were going to convince me it was all a misunderstanding."

"There was no misunderstanding. I stole him." Reaching out, he took her hand in his. "There was a good reason."

"Oh, Max," she said, swept up in a sense of despair.

"Let me tell you how it came to be."

She nodded, willing to hear him out. But tears were threatening and she knew he could tell. "Please," she said shakily.

He nodded, then took his hand away from hers and stared at the wall. "While I was living in Mercuria, I rented a room from a family, the Minderts, who had once been quite wealthy but through one thing and another, had lost all their money. All they had left from the old days, besides their house and land, was a stable of three beautiful, award-winning palomino horses, and it took all Dirk Mindert's efforts to make enough to keep them fed and well taken care of."

His eyes were troubled as he remembered how it had been for these people. "The whole family had one goal—keep those horses. But while I was living there, they had to get rid of two of them. They just couldn't keep up with expenses. They were about to lose their house and they couldn't...." He shook his head as though the words just wouldn't come for a moment.

"I would have tried to help them, but the Mercurian government wasn't paying me at the time. So I didn't have much in the way of resources." He looked down at his hands. They were clenched into fists. Slowly, he made them relax.

"But we managed to get together enough money to keep the most important one, a beautiful horse named Belle. He belonged to the Minderts' eight-year-old daughter, Mindy. She rode her every day. It was magical to watch the way she and that huge horse had a rapport between them. It would have been a crime to separate them."

Kayla murmured something and reached for his hand again. His fingers curled around hers, but he didn't seem to know it. He was wrapped up in his story.

"The public affairs minister and I had a falling out. Bottom line, he hated me. He tried to undercut me a couple of ways that just didn't work out. And then, all of a sudden, he took Mindy's horse away." His voice deepened roughly. "He had some trumped-up national security reason. They were supposedly confiscating all horses in the sector."

He turned to look into her eyes. "It was a bunch of bull. I went to him to try to get it rescinded. He called the guard, tried to have me arrested." He shrugged. "I got away." He gazed at the wall again and took a deep breath. "I found out where they were keeping Belle and I stole her back. I took her and I rode her right across the border."

He looked back at Kayla as though to see how she was taking that. She looked right back. So far, she wished he hadn't done it, but she didn't see how it was going to be a capital offense. These things could be explained…couldn't they? Maybe Pellea could authorize a payment?

But Max was still telling his story.

"I managed to have the Minderts meet me. They were about to lose their land anyway. It was time for them to go. I got them out of the country and on their way to Switzerland. They have family there." He took a deep breath and looked at her. "And Mindy has her horse back."

"Oh. I'm glad. But…" It did seem a large price to pay for a horse. She admired him for his instincts to help, but… "Max, you could go to prison for this." Not only that, but he could also be giving up his place in the royal family.

"Yes," he said simply. "I might." He stared hard into her eyes, his own silver with passion. "But, Kayla, I don't really care. There was something more important than that involved. And I would do it again. I would do it tomorrow."

CHAPTER SIX

MAX's hand tightened on Kayla's. "You see, there's more to this story. Mindy is a sweet and adorable girl. You would love her. But more than that, Mindy…" His voice choked a bit and he cleared his throat. "Mindy is blind, you see. Belle was her life companion, her only joy. You understand?" He searched her eyes, looking very serious.

She drew her breath in sharply, and then she nodded slowly. She did understand. She had to admit, Mindy's blindness made all the difference. The fact that he had thrown away everything he had in order to help the child…she was touched by what he'd done. "Yes. I think so. I do understand."

He nodded, as though satisfied with her answer and by what he could see in her eyes. "Good. It had to be done."

She stared at him. Yes, it had to be done. And he'd done it. He was a man who went ahead and did things. He didn't wait to see how the wind might blow. He made things happen. Suddenly, her heart filled with affection for him. So he stole a horse—so what!

"And you...?" she asked.

He shook his head. "I never went back. It was time for me to go anyway."

She took a deep breath and sighed as though she'd just been through something important. "Wow. You were a hero."

"No." He shook his head and appeared pained. "It was my fault the horse was taken in the first place. I should have been more obsequious to the minister. I don't ever seem to be able to learn that lesson."

"And I don't suppose you were much of a hero to the Mercurian regime, were you?"

He gave a short laugh. "Hardly."

"So by the time you left, they already had a pretty deep grudge against you."

"So it seems."

Their tea was getting cold and the first round of sandwiches had arrived. Luckily, they were delicious and Kayla began to relax. It was wonderful what a little bit of tea and some yummy finger food could do. She was feeling so much better about everything.

He had reasons for taking the plane and reasons for stealing the horse. Surely he also had an explanation for the historical artifact. Whatever that was. But she wouldn't bug him about that right now. All in good time.

She definitely wouldn't let herself get caught up in so much worry about it any longer. She had work to do. She was supposed to mold him into a prince in a week. It was time to get going on that little job.

"We've got to get back to the essential things we've been tasked with," she told him between bites of a watercress delectable. She gave him a significant look. "Prince lessons."

He rolled his eyes but didn't balk. "I'm game," he said with resignation. "What do I do next? Cut my hair in a pageboy?"

"Nothing so old-fashioned as that," she assured him. "But I think we ought to make a list." She pulled a notebook out of her huge purse. She'd brought it along just for this sort of thing.

"A list?" His look was wary.

"A list of all the things the modern nobleman must be."

He gave her a crooked grin so endearing, she felt something move in her chest. He'd grinned at her with just that look before. She had a quick flashback to a day on the beach down on the Mediterranean, a day so bright and beautiful, it made her think her world had been enchanted. Max and Eddie were competing to see who could build the best sand castle. And she was just sitting to the side, watching them and laughing at their silly macho banter. The sea was turquoise blue, the sand was sparkling, the sun was liquid gold.

A perfect day. A perfect time. A bittersweet sense of nostalgia swept through her and she had to hold back tears. Nothing would ever be so special again.

She pulled herself back into the now and Max was still making fun of her list.

"I'll see your modern nobleman list," he teased her. "And then we'll raise the stakes and make a list of everything the non-noble should know before attempting to play the royal game. That one I might be able to shoot for."

She shook her head. "Don't worry. This doesn't mean you have to absorb everything all at once. It's more of a wish list." She wrote on the top of the page, The Attributes of the Perfect Prince.

"Perfect?" He groaned. "Might as well toss it right now."

"Will you stop it?" she said, raising her pen to her cheek as she thought things over. "I know. We'll start with physical appearance."

He seemed surprised. "You don't think I've got the looks for the job?"

She flashed him a satirical glance. "As far as the basics, you'll do. But there's more to it. There's a certain way that a prince carries himself."

He grinned. "Arrogance and disdain? I think I can handle that."

She pretended to glare at him. "No. Confidence and competence mixed with a certain sense of approachability. Leadership and the common touch, all wrapped up in one handsome package." She wrinkled her nose. "Do you understand what I mean?"

He looked back and then sighed. "I think I get it."

"Good." She nodded. "Work on that, please."

"Oh, sure. No problem."

"And then there is your manner of dress."

He looked down at his casual shirt and Levi's and eyed her questioningly.

Her look back was scathing and she shook her head. "I'll get together some pictures to show you what you can do on that."

"Spend money," he said cynically.

"Yes. But carefully. I'll teach you the tricks."

"No kidding?" His smile was nothing if not provocative. "I didn't know you had a few of those up your sleeve."

She grinned back and tapped him with her pen. "Be ready for anything."

"Oh, I will."

"But right now," she said, shifting gears and getting serious again, "I want to see how you walk."

He blinked at her. "What?"

"Your walk. Is it royal enough? Does it

need more backbone? Insouciance? Perhaps a bit more savoir faire?"

"Listen, I'll do anything you want, but I'm not going French."

She laughed. "You only wish you could be French. The French know how to walk."

"I've never been put down for my walk before."

"Let's see it, then."

He blinked at her. She couldn't mean what she seemed to mean. Could she? "What?"

She gestured for him to stand. "Do it."

His eyes were clouded. "Do what?"

She leaned toward him, holding back a laugh at his hesitancy. "Walk across the room. Let's see what you've got."

"Here? Now?" He looked around the room, his face worried.

"Yes, here and now." She bit back a grin and decided it was time to take pity on him. "Oh, don't worry. Something simple. Just a quick turn and back again."

She almost laughed out loud at the look he gave her. It was obvious the whole concept was a huge embarrassment to him.

Funny. Had he never been conscious of how he came across before?

"Just get up and walk over to the counter and pick up a tray of sweets and bring them back here. No one will know you're on display."

He took a deep breath, his look as close to a glare as she'd ever received from him. "All right," he said grudgingly. "But be kind."

Rising, he threw her an exasperated glance and started across the room. His walk was slow, strong and controlled and she knew right away there was nothing she could suggest to improve it. The set of his shoulders, the tilt of his head, the length of his stride—his manner of carrying himself might not be particularly royal, but it was about as good as it could get.

And then she noticed something odd. It was like a force field moving through the room. Every single woman, even those who couldn't have possibly seen him get up from where they were sitting, was turning her head in his direction. What was he—magnetized? She watched, eyes wide and hand over her mouth, as he picked up the tray and started back. They were all staring.

And it wasn't that he was so handsome. There were other handsome men in the room. There was more to it than that. There was a sense about him—a little bit of danger, a little bit of bravado and a lot of something else. She bit her lip, trying to analyze just what it was. Those gorgeous eyes seemed to say he knew things other people didn't—secret things about life and love. And whatever those secret things were, they seemed to draw the attention of every female imagination in the place.

"Wow," she breathed as he sat down again.

He lifted a dark eyebrow sardonically. "I was that good, was I?"

She rolled her eyes. "No," she told him briskly, not willing to let him know the power he had, just in case he wasn't sure of it yet. "I was just thinking what a lot of work we have ahead of us."

He winced and looked rebellious. "I can save everybody the trouble and forget the whole thing," he offered, only half joking. "If even the way I walk isn't good enough…"

"Isn't good enough," she echoed weakly, shaking her head. It was no use. He might as well know the truth. "Someone should call out the paramedics," she whispered to him wryly, leaning close so as not to be overheard. "Half the women in here are about to swoon right off their chairs after watching you walk across the room."

He eyed her skeptically, a cloudy, slightly bewildered expression in his eyes. Then he spoke with such honesty, she was taken aback. "Kayla, come on. Don't mess with my self-confidence like that. I'm feeling shaky enough about this whole royal thing. I don't need you, of all people, to be mocking me."

She recoiled in surprise. She hadn't meant to do that. She hadn't thought anything could ruffle his famously appealing feathers. Evidently, he wasn't quite as cocky as he seemed. To think that he had never noticed the effect he had on women was a revelation.

"I'm sorry," she said quickly. "I'm just as new at this as you are. I was trying to stick to a light tone and I guess I went a little too far." Reaching across the table, she took his hand in hers and leaned forward, looking into his eyes earnestly. "Max, you've got a great walk. Manly and noble and full of confidence. At least, that's the way it comes across and that is what counts. You were born to be a prince, no matter how you want to fight it. It's in your blood."

He squeezed her hand and didn't answer, but his eyes were smiling.

"But we aren't finished," she added quickly. "There are a lot of superficial things you need to learn. We still have a long way to go."

He nodded, agreeing with her. "'And miles to go before we sleep,'" he said softly.

She gasped and smiled. "A literary quote. Very good. Knowing good poetry is a real plus in a prince."

"Eddie taught me that one." His eyes clouded. "Too bad it wasn't Eddie who got the chance to be a prince. He would have done a bang-up job of it, wouldn't he?"

As she watched him, something caught in her heart. "Max, Eddie was great. I miss him constantly. It just kills me that he had to die. But…" And here was the hard part. It was true, but hard to say. "Max, he was no better a person than you are."

Max winced as though she'd slapped him. "Don't say that. Of course he was."

"No." She shook her head. "He wasn't perfect. He was a man, just like you are. He had his good days and his bad ones." She tried to smile. "He could be darn grumpy when the weather didn't suit him. You remember."

A slow grin erased Max's frown. "I remember."

Their gazes met and held. Max began to lean closer, his eyes filling with smoky memories.

"Kayla," he began huskily.

But he never got any further. A shriek filled the room, a sound like a fire engine coming through, and they both jumped back, startled.

"Oh, no," Kayla said as she leaped to her feet and whirled. And just in time. A child who could barely toddle was racing toward her as fast as his chubby little legs could take him.

"Teddy!"

He threw himself at her, practically flying through the air, and she caught him and pulled him up into her arms, half laughing, half scolding. "Teddy, what are you doing here?"

"I am so sorry," Caroline said, rushing in behind him with her own little boy in her arms. "We saw you through the glass. And once he knew his mom was in here, there was no stopping him. He climbed right out of the stroller!"

Holding Teddy in her arms was like being close to heaven and Kayla always reveled in it. But there was another emotion lurking. Guilt. Leaving her baby with someone else was something she had to do, but the guilt never completely left her, no matter how busy and involved she was at work. She held him tightly and whispered soothing words against his adorable head, and he whimpered and pressed in close. And the guilt welled up inside her.

She looked up, realizing there were other issues that had to be dealt with. Her sister was smiling at Max, but she hadn't told her anything about him and she obviously had no idea who he was.

"Caroline, this is an old friend from back in my Trialta days. Max Arragen. He…he and Eddie were really close. They flew together.…"

"Nice to meet you." Caroline frowned as she held out her hand for his. "Wait. Max Arragen? Aren't you…?"

He gave her one of his devastating self-deprecating smiles. "The new prince. Yes."

Caroline's eyes lit up. "Congratulations," she said, glancing at Kayla. "I had no idea. Wow. You must be really excited with all this hoopla."

"Oh, yeah. Something like that anyway."

"I feel like I should do a little curtsy or something."

"No. Please." He seemed genuinely embarrassed and she laughed.

Kayla watched them and she had to smile. Her sister resembled her quite a bit, but her blond hair was cut short and perky. Caroline was the friendly, outgoing sort, while Kayla had always felt she was the shy one, the quietly competent one whose work no one really noticed. And yet, here she was, having lunch with a prince, working for the queen… Maybe it was time to reassess her self-image.

"Ma-ma," Teddy said, tugging on her collar and adding something indecipherable that probably meant, *Let's get out of here and have some 'mommy and me' time together.*

The words weren't there but Kayla heard the message loud and clear. She looked up at Max, waiting for him to finish chatting with her sister and notice the baby.

"We were on our way to the playground," Caroline was saying. "If you two have any lunch hour left, why don't you come along?"

Kayla looked at Max. He was staring at Teddy. Her heart began to race. What was he seeing? What did those sharp eyes catch? What were the vibes that were getting through to his instinctive reactions?

It was hard to tell. He was smiling, but something in that smile was beginning to stiffen up. Had he noticed? Had he taken a quick assessment of whom Teddy might look like? It was an exercise that was completely familiar to her. She'd done it periodically ever since her baby was born.

She was blond with dark eyes. Eddie had been the same. But Max had dark bronzed hair and shockingly blue eyes. And so did Teddy.

It didn't mean anything. Of course it didn't. There were all sorts of combinations possible with the logic of genetics. She knew that. He knew that. But still…

"This is Teddy," she told him, wishing her voice wasn't shaking. "Teddy, this is Max. Say 'hi.'" She made him wave, but his little baby face was rebellious.

Max hesitated. He didn't seem to have much experience socializing with babies and in the end, he smiled awkwardly and said, "Hi, Teddy."

Teddy turned and hid his face against her neck. Kayla searched Max's eyes, trying to guess what he might be thinking. She didn't see any clues. But she also didn't see the sort of appreciation for her beautiful child that she might have expected.

"I think he's tired," she said, knowing it sounded like an excuse.

"Oh, sure," Caroline chimed in helpfully. "He didn't have a nap this morning and he usually goes down for a half hour or so."

Teddy still had morning naps? Had she really been out of his daily routine for so long that she didn't know it any longer? She felt a sudden sense of remorse. She should be with her baby today. He needed her. She needed him. He was clinging to her and she was getting the message.

As she pulled him closer, he turned to look at Max. Teddy's expression didn't change, but his lower lip thrust out and his little hands dug deeper into the fabric of her blouse. *This is my mom*, his face said. *She belongs to me.*

"Cute kid," Max said shortly, but there was no warmth in his eyes as he turned away.

Kayla made her decision. "I think we're going to have to put off doing more work on our prince project," she told him. "I really feel I need to go to the playground with them. I've been neglecting Teddy so much lately. Do you…do you want to come along?"

She waited as he mulled it over, hoping he would say no.

"I've got a few things I've got to take care of," he said at last, his gaze touching hers, then veering off again. "I'll catch you later."

"Okay." Relief flooded her. This was just too nerve-wracking to keep up much longer.

She didn't look at Max again. Her attention was all for her baby. Caroline gave her a questioning look and she knew that her sister wanted to get filled in on a few details and get a fix on her feelings, but she wasn't up to discussing Max and all that he meant to her. Too much had happened too soon and she needed to reevaluate.

But right now it was Teddy's time. She turned her face away and began a baby-talk discussion with her son. Her sister would have to wait.

Max wandered down into the main castle courtyard and out along the man-made miniwilderness where he could lose himself among the trees. A small babbling brook ran cheerfully past a large flat rock, and that was where he settled, out of sight of the walkways.

Normally, he wasn't much for introspection. He thought of himself as a man of action. He didn't tend to second-guess himself, to try to analyze why he did the things he went through or why the results had been good or bad. Navel gazing was just not his style.

But today he felt like a little self-analysis was in order. He'd just spent an hour in a meeting with two of his brothers—Prince Mykal, who had been identified as one of the royals only a few weeks before Max had, and Prince David, who had caught sight of him in the hallway and invited him to join them in a discussion of renovations to a still-destroyed area of the castle.

Much of the original and ancient castle had been burned on the night thirty years before when the Granvilli family had mounted a successful rebellion and taken over Ambria, killing the king and queen and establishing their vicious dictatorial regime. That night, each of the royal children had been spirited away by various servants or friends or members of the administration and hidden from the Granvillis. It had taken twenty-five years for the princes and princess to begin to find each other again. Their fight to win back their country had been successful and now there was only a remnant of the Granvilli faction that held a remote part of the island to deal with.

David was the second oldest prince and considered second only to King Monte in importance. Tall and dark, he had a serious air about him.

"Max, I'm glad to see you," he said when he met his brother in the hall. "I've been neglecting you, I know. There are so many issues coming up right now. I really want to get you more involved in management matters. We all have to share the burden of managing the castle, and eventually, the nation at large." He gave him a firm pat on the back. "I'm meeting Mykal in the blue meeting room right now. Why don't you join us?"

Max was glad to do just that. He was still new enough at the castle to be a little starstruck by his brothers and he wasn't sure he would ever get over being impressed by them. He'd been told a little of David's background. He'd been raised by a family in the Netherlands, and since he was six when he was taken, he remembered where he'd come from. But he also knew it had to be kept secret, and it wasn't until he was in his twenties that he and Monte found each other and began to plot their return to power. As the two oldest, they were regularly considered the head and heart of the family.

Mykal was almost as new to this as Max was, and it showed. Still recovering from a terrible motorcycle accident, he had trouble sitting for long, and by the time an hour had passed it was obvious the meeting had to be adjourned for the day.

But Max sat with them at the long, shiny table and made small talk about how he was settling in. Then the real work of the meeting had begun, and he was very quickly over his head. The talk was all architectural plans and cost estimates and zoning regulations, things he had never dealt with before. He listened carefully and filed information away to learn more about later. But he was definitely out of his element, and what's more, though he liked and admired them, he didn't feel any special connection. They were brothers, but it didn't feel the way he had expected that sort of relationship to feel. When they all rose, shook hands and parted ways, his head was swimming.

That feeling was still with him now. He was glad to have carved out an hour to be on his own. There was a lot to think about. He was feeling a bit shaky about what he ought to be doing and generally undecided about his own future. Bottom line—what the hell was he doing here living in a castle?

The whole prince thing just didn't feel right. He'd never asked for it. He'd been happily flying reconnaissance missions over the Granvilli territory when he'd been called in to the commander's office and asked to take a battery of tests. He still didn't know who had nominated him for testing or why.

If only he'd refused and walked away right at that point, none of this would be happening. He'd be off flying in someone else's war.

Still, what was stopping him from doing exactly what he pleased right now? He could go. He could find someone else to fly for. He would keep his promise to the queen, but once that was over, he wasn't so sure he was going to stick around. After all, what was really keeping him here?

Right now, he would have to say it was mostly Kayla. He hadn't expected to find her here, but now that they had reconnected, he knew he didn't want to lose her again.

Kayla was important to him. She always would be. He remembered those days in Trialta as the best days of his life. He and Eddie had hit it off like brothers, born to be together, and Kayla had been a huge part of that bond.

Funny. When he'd heard she had a child, he'd assumed her baby would be an extension of that. That he would love the kid as a small form of Eddie. But the reality hadn't fit in with the vision. There was something about that baby...

He was definitely a beautiful baby boy. But looking at him, something hadn't felt right. Something about the kid bothered him, made him want to look away quickly, and he didn't want to feel that way about Kayla's baby. Very strange. Maybe he ought to stay away from the kid until he was a little older.

A twig snapped and he turned his head, sure someone was coming into his little clearing. He didn't want company. He stared into the brush, ready to scowl a nonwelcome. But no one appeared. He stared harder, his gaze darting from one gap in the greenery to another, looking for movement. Nothing. Funny…he was sure he'd heard someone.

And it had happened before. He remembered getting the same feeling when he was wandering through the halls, earlier. A feeling that he wasn't alone.

Suddenly he had a prickly feeling on the back of his neck, and he stood, turning slowly, hands balled into fists. Yes, damn it, someone was watching him. Maybe he couldn't see it, but he sure as hell could feel it.

CHAPTER SEVEN

KAYLA looked up, startled, as Max came into the office. There was a thunderstorm brewing in that handsome face.

"Max," she said, but he walked right past her desk and confronted Pellea.

"I want to know why you've got somebody following me," he said curtly. "Don't you trust me? Has it really come to this?"

Pellea looked up and gaped at him, bewildered and showing it. "What are you talking about?"

"Look, I've made you a promise. I may be unreliable in superficial ways, but when I make a promise, I keep it. There was no call for you to send spies to watch over me. I don't like it."

She was shaking her head, looking at him as though he'd lost his mind. "I don't have anyone following you," she protested earnestly. "Really, Max. I swear."

His anger seemed to pulse in the small room. He took a deep breath, trying to calm himself. He knew he was over-the-top and taking it out on Pellea wasn't going to fix anything. This wasn't really her fault. He'd been angry when he thought it was, but her outrage told him differently, and he began to cool down. If he were honest with himself, he knew his own doubts and insecurities were more to blame for this outburst than anything the queen could have done. He needed to get a grip.

"I was just down in the courtyard, in among the trees, and someone was there watching me. I know it."

She shrugged. "There may have been someone watching you, but I didn't tell them to. Believe me, Max. I wouldn't do that." She made a face. "Not yet, anyway."

He looked at the ground and shook his head. For someone trying to learn to act like a prince, he was doing a lousy job of it. He looked up with a rueful smile and made a slight bow toward her.

"Your Majesty, please forgive me. This

was rude and uncalled for. I had no right to attack you like this and I'm sorry."

Pellea's smile lit up the room. It seemed she knew earnest regret when she saw it. "Of course I forgive you. This is not supposed to be a fight. We're both on the same side." She rose from her desk chair and came out to throw her arms around him and then kiss him on both cheeks.

"Listen to me," he told her. "I will make you a pledge right now. I won't do anything behind your back. If anything happens, I'll tell you. If I decide I have to leave, I'll tell you. No secrets."

She nodded. "Good." One last pat on his cheek and she turned. "And in the spirit of openness, sit down. I'll give you the rundown on our latest outreach to Mercuria."

He sank into a chair across from her, but glanced back at Kayla. She gave him a wink and a tiny approving smile. Ridiculously, he suddenly felt much better.

"All right, here's the news. We've sent our ambassador to Mercuria."

Max nodded. "And what message does he take with him?"

Pellea shuffled papers on her desk and

brought up the pertinent ones. "In answer to their charges, we respond thusly—it is our understanding that the airplane was given to Prince Maximillian, formerly known as Max Arragen, in payment for his help in establishing the Mercurian Air Force and therefore not an item that can be reclaimed."

She looked up for his approval, and he nodded.

"As for the horse, we made it clear that we feel there was a misunderstanding and a wrong done to the horse's owner, who now has regained possession of the horse. If they like, we are prepared to pay damages for the loss of it to the Mercurian government." She nodded toward Kayla. "I've had that whole episode explained to me. Kayla repeated what you told her this morning."

He glanced back at Kayla again and nodded. "Sounds reasonable."

"As for the historical artifact, I let them know that we have no idea what this might be or how it might have come into your possession. We shall await clarification.

Barring that, we are unwilling to count that as a serious charge against you."

"Wow. I'd say that pretty much covers all the bases."

Pellea nodded. "Now we wait to see how they take it. We should have their response tomorrow." She gave him a significant look. "And then, we'll see."

He heard the warning in her voice. She was seriously worried about this.

"You've said the Mercurians were a big help in the fight to regain Ambria for the DeAngelis royal family," he said musingly. "What made them come in on your side?"

Pellea shrugged. "As you know, Mercuria is a tiny stretch of land along the coast, not even as large or as important to this area as Ambria, whose main source of wealth comes from tourists, mainly in gambling. Some wags have called it nothing more than a casino with a nice beach. But they have been traditional allies of ours, and the fact that they have a monarchy, just as we do, cemented our ties more recently."

He nodded. "And they are the closest country to you, aren't they?"

"Yes. Just an hour by boat will bring you right to the foot of the Mercurian castle. You could almost consider them a neighbor."

"Do you know King Juomo personally?"

"No, I don't. I guess the families had personal ties back in the dark ages, but as far as I know, none of us have come face-to-face with any of them. As I understand it, they are rather reclusive."

He nodded. "Yes. Very reclusive. And very strange."

"So I've heard." She made a face. "That doesn't bode well. It's hard to judge how they will take this. What do you think?"

He shook his head. "I have no idea. King Juomo liked me, until he didn't like me anymore. And I'm not sure what made the change."

"Oh, well." Pellea waved a hand dismissively. "We shall see. And I need to get back to work." She smiled at him. "Cheer up. We'll get through this."

He smiled back. "Of course." Taking a deep breath, he rose, took his leave of the queen and pivoted to Kayla.

"Do you have time to go get a cup of

coffee with me?" he asked, looking at her without any clear emotion.

She glanced at Pellea, who nodded her permission, and smiled. "Sure," she said, reaching to pull her tiny clutch purse out of her larger bag. "I won't be long," she promised the queen.

She almost had to run to keep up with Max's stride once they were out in the walkway. His walk was strong and aggressive, with a hint of residual anger still hovering over his mood.

"Will you tell me why you're so upset?" she asked.

He gave her a sideways glance and didn't respond as they came out onto the public corridor and up to the coffee bistro. It was packed with people and the lines were long.

"There's a vending machine a little farther out this way. We can get coffee and go out on the balcony."

They got their coffee in paper cups from the machine and made their way outside. The balcony was small, but there was a table flanked by two chairs, and they went to it after a quick look over the railing. The blue skies were gone and a cool wind blustered in and out of the crevices and still neither of them had said a word.

Max stared down into his coffee. She watched him. Finally he looked up and met her gaze.

"You know what?" he said. "I want to go."

Her heart jumped. His eyes looked hard and unhappy.

"Where?" she said.

He shrugged. "Away. Anywhere. Something new. Something different." His blue eyes held hers. "This isn't the life for me."

"Max…" She reached for his hand and held it tightly.

"I don't feel like I belong here. I don't think the way these people do. My instincts don't work here. I really feel I need to go."

"Max…"

His wide eyes stared right into her soul. "Will you go with me?"

She stared at him. How could he ask such a thing? Didn't he realize she had a life here? A son? She couldn't go anywhere she felt like. She had commitments.

He could read her refusal in her eyes. The child. Of course. What was he thinking? She had the child. He pulled his hand away and looked out at the grey skies.

A cold wind blew in and Kayla shivered.

"Here, take this," he said, slipping out of the denim jacket and handing it to her. "Unless you still scorn it?" he tried to tease, his smile unconvincingly stiff.

"I never scorned it," she protested, shrugging into it and huddling gratefully in the warmth his body had left inside. "I love jeans jackets."

"Just not on princes."

She pulled the jacket in close and looked at him. "Not true. Max, I know you want to wear the clothes you feel comfortable in. And you should be able to. But you have to know what's expected of you in certain situations. That's all. We're not trying to change the fundamental you."

He grunted, and she leaned closer. "Tomorrow we'll go clothes shopping and I'll show you what I mean."

He stared at her and finally a smile began to tug at the corners of his mouth. "I guess that means you don't think much of my plan to leave," he said, eyes smiling sadly.

"I think it stinks. You promised Pellea two weeks. You'll manage to stick it out that long. I know you. You won't run."

He wasn't so sure she knew him as well as she thought she did. Running was what he'd done all his life—running from his problems, running from expectations, running from commitment. He knew it was time for him to grow up and stop running, but he wasn't sure how to do that.

"You won't run," she repeated confidently, and he merely smiled and let her think she had him pegged.

"At least you won't really need new clothes tonight," she mentioned. "Pellea has a dinner planned for all you princes, but it's beer and pizza and football on the television."

His smile evaporated in an instant. This was the first he'd heard about it. He scowled, but she wasn't cowed.

"You need to interact with your brothers more," she said. "Once you get to know them better, you'll feel more welcome here."

"Maybe." He didn't look convinced, but the sun came out from behind a cloud at that very moment, and it was as though liquid gold was streaming down all around them.

She laughed and went to the railing, enjoying the warmth of the sun, and he followed. The countryside around the castle looked magical. It was late afternoon and the shadows were long and colors intensified.

"Do you ever go walking down by the stream?" he asked her, pointing it out below.

"No, I've never been there."

He grabbed her hand. "Let's go," he said spontaneously. "You'll love it."

They took the elevator down and walked quickly through the corridors and onto the back patio, hoping to catch as much sunshine as they could before the cloud cover took over again. He took her hand and led her through the trees to his favorite rock. She scanned the area, enchanted with the rustling leaves and babbling brook. Then she got a thoughtful look.

"Is this where you were when you thought you were being watched?" she said accusingly.

"Yes, it is." He looked excessively innocent. "Why do you ask?"

"You just wanted me to come down here to see if I could help you catch the culprits, didn't you?" She pretended to take a swipe at him.

He laughed. "No," he said, fending off her mock attack and grabbing her wrists. "Though come to think of it, two sets of eyes are better than one."

He pulled her close until their faces were within inches of each other. She smiled into his eyes. He smiled back and something electric happened. He was going to kiss her. She could feel it. Her breath caught in her throat and she pulled back quickly, heart pounding.

"I don't see anybody," she said breathlessly. "I don't hear anybody. I think you're getting paranoid."

"No. Someone was there." He pulled her back against him. "But I don't care anymore."

He saw alarm in her eyes—denial, dismissal and a lot of worry, but like he'd said, he didn't care anymore. His mouth took hers as though he had a right to it, as though he'd gone through all the reasons why she wasn't his for the kissing and decided to throw them out the window. He wanted her. He'd always wanted her. And now that he had her in his arms, he needed to feel her heat, taste her warm sweetness, touch her beautiful body.

His hands slid under the jacket, under her sweater, up her slender back and she arched her softness against his hard chest. His kiss was hungry and hot and she answered it back the same way. The wind swirled around them. Leaves blew around their feet. The water from the brook sang a happy song, and time seemed to stand still.

It was meant to be a short kiss, just something quick and loaded with commitment and affection, but he never wanted it to stop. If it had been up to him, it never would have. But she knew it couldn't last.

"Max."

He was kissing the curve of her neck, tasting her skin, devouring her sweetness.

"Max!"

Pulling back, he looked at her groggily. She was laughing.

"Max, stop!"

He shook his head, then groaned and let her go. Running his fingers through his hair, he tried to get his balance back.

"Sorry," he muttered. "You just feel so good. I want to hold you forever."

She looked into his eyes, smiling, loving him, but not sure what to say. They couldn't do this. He couldn't kiss her this way. There was something intoxicating between the two of them. Once they started, they didn't seem to know how to stop. Reaching out, she cupped his rough cheek in her hand and smiled sadly.

And then, without a word, she stepped away carefully and sank down to sit on the rock. He followed and sat beside her.

"Eddie would have loved this place," he said softly, and then winced, wishing he'd kept his mouth shut.

She didn't look at him. She didn't say a word, but he knew she what she was thinking.

They were silent for a few minutes, watching the water, and then Max started talking about his brothers again, haltingly at first. And then he just kept going, talking as though they had never stopped.

"You know, there's a big difference between me and the other princes," he said at one point. "They all grew up in families. They might not have been the right families, but at least they had that. I think I'm the only one who sort of got thrown out with the trash."

His words might have been bitter, but she was glad to notice that his tone was more bemused.

"Actually," she told him, "Prince Cassius—the one we all call Joe—had a pretty rough time of it as well."

"Prince Joe? The surfer prince?" He had to grin. He'd met Joe.

She nodded, smiling. "That's him. Whoever was supposed to hide him that night didn't show up and the kitchen maid ended up taking him with her when she ran, hiding him under her shawl on the boat. She didn't know what to do with him, so she took him back home to England, whereupon she promptly died and left him to be raised by members of her family who had no clue who he was."

"How did he end up in California?"

"The family emigrated and then the parents got divorced and they all pretty much split up. I guess it wasn't much of a warm-and-toasty family after all. Sort of dysfunctional. The way I heard it, he took off pretty young and then he joined the military."

Max nodded. "Okay. Joe and I might just have a little bit in common. Maybe I'll have a chance to talk to him tonight." He made a comical face. "Pizza and beer," he repeated, shaking his head. "I guess she really does want to make me feel at home. That's practically my daily diet as it is."

"She's doing her best." She looked at him whimsically. "I don't think you realize how much better this is going to make things for you," she said simply.

He groaned and the anger flared in him again. That was the last thing he wanted to hear.

"Don't tell me how wonderful this is for me and how it's going to change my life. I don't want my life changed. I like things the way they've been. I don't want to be a prince."

She was frowning at him now. "You don't want to be a prince because you don't want to have to conform to rules and standards. You don't think anyone else should have a say in how you should act, do you?"

He blinked, not used to tough talk from her. "So? What's wrong with that?"

Her eyes flashed. "Grow up, Max. It's time for you to stop playing at life and start living it."

Maybe I don't want to.

He didn't say it. The words popped out onto the tip of his tongue, but he wisely held them back, and as he thought them over, he realized how childish they were. What the hell. She was right. It was time for him to grow up. Grabbing her hand, he pressed his lips to the center of her palm, then looked up at her, smiling.

"How did I do without you all this time?" he said huskily. "Eddie once said to me that if anything ever happened to you, he wouldn't want to go on alone. And I can see why."

His words sent a shock through her. She closed her eyes and thought about them for a moment. Then she looked at him, trying not to be resentful. "And you're wondering how I've managed to go on so normally without him?"

"No," he said, looking shocked at the thought. "That isn't what I meant to say at all."

"Then why did you say it?"

He shook his head, trying to remember what had been in his mind at the time. "I just wanted to remind you to remember how much Eddie loved you."

She pulled her arms in close. "I don't need reminding. I remember very well. I remember it all the time." She still felt resentful as she looked at him. "I didn't get to where I am without a lot of pain, you know."

He nodded, searching her face, staring into her eyes. "I know that, Kayla. There was enough pain to go around." He winced and looked away. "I felt it, too. After Eddie died, I went a little crazy for a while."

"Didn't we all?"

"No, I mean it." He looked back at her. "I took stupid chances, did stupid things. In some ways, it almost felt as though I couldn't live life normally anymore. If a guy as super as Eddie could get killed like that, what right did I have to be happy?" He frowned, remembering. "I began to make careless mistakes. At one point, I did something stupid and I had to ditch my plane. I bailed out in time, but it was a while before they found me." He shook his head. "That woke me up."

"That was when I saw the report on the news. I…I really thought you were gone, too."

He nodded. "It was hard to accept a world where the best people got snuffed out like candles. No real reason. Just here one moment, gone the next. To see a good guy like Eddie get killed so easily and a waster like I am get lucky every time—it didn't seem right. I was having a hard time with that."

"Max, Eddie's gone. I don't think you've completely faced it yet."

"Have you?"

"Yes. I've tried very hard. There's a part of me that will always love him and miss him horribly. But most of life has to go on without him. I either go on or I throw myself off the balcony."

His eyes darkened with horror. "You wouldn't do that."

"No. I couldn't do that. I have Teddy."

He looked startled, as though he'd forgotten.

"Teddy is my whole life now," she told him carefully, wishing she saw a smile or a look of affection or something friendly toward her son. How could this man not feel something? "Do you understand that?"

"Yeah, I think I do."

She thought about the fact that he'd never really lived in a family. Maybe he didn't understand what it meant to have a child, how it consumed your soul. It was true that as far as she could see, he didn't react well to Teddy and she didn't know why. But maybe this was a part of it.

Or maybe it was something else, something about Teddy's background that threw him off. And if that was what it was, she knew she didn't want to face that at all.

"I've got to get back."

He nodded. "I'll walk with you."

They started off and once again, they both fell silent, as if they had talked about things that needed some mulling over before they mentioned them to each other again. At the door to her office, Kayla smiled at him.

"Could I come by and see you tonight?" he asked. "After the pizza party?"

Her smile disappeared. "No," she said slowly, thinking it over on the run. "I think it would be better if we kept our relationship on a completely professional level. Forget that we're friends."

He looked as though he thought she was nuts. "Forget that we're friends?" He shook his head, his anger beginning to hint at a return engagement. "No. That's carrying things too far. I'll be circumspect during prince lessons, but once they're over, you're fair game."

"Fair game?" she repeated, puzzled.

"You got it. You can run but you can't hide."

"What are you talking about?"

"This." Taking her face in his hands, he bent down and kissed her softly. His lips were warm and his solid male earthy scent made her head spin. His kiss was sweet and sincere and somehow much more effective than the wild one out by the little river. It brought tears to her eyes and left her gasping, aching for more.

"And that's just a sample of things to

come," he told her, giving her a triumphant grin and turning to go.

Speechless, she watched him go, her cheeks burning. It wasn't until he was out of sight that she remembered she still had his jacket.

She was fixing Teddy a nice peanut butter sandwich for dinner, because that was all he would eat besides eggs and bananas. He was dancing around the apartment, bobbing his head and pretending to play a little plastic guitar, when the phone rang.

"Hey, it's me."

Amazing how his voice could send sparkles through her bloodstream. She remembered the kisses and the sparkles intensified.

"Max. What is it?"

He paused, listening. "What's that noise in the background?"

"Oh, it's just Teddy. He's so funny. I wish you could see him. He's sort of singing and dancing and banging things. But you may ignore at will. Go on."

"He makes a lot of noise for such a small kid."

"You don't know the half of it," she said, laughing. "He's only just begun."

"Hmm."

Once again Kayla got the impression that he didn't like her baby much, and she frowned.

"Well, I just called to tell you my place has been totally ransacked."

"What? How did someone get by the guard?"

There was an extensive network of security in the castle, but it was especially concentrated in the royal wing.

"That's a good question."

"Did they take anything?"

"I don't think so."

"What were they after?"

He paused, then said, "I think it's all related. The people watching me, the people going through my things. What do you think?"

"It would seem logical I guess. But you have no idea who they are, right?"

"Right. Still, I think it's related to this. Now if I could figure out what they're looking for…"

"How about an historical artifact from

Mercuria?" she suggested, eyes widening as she thought of it.

"I was thinking the same thing." He paused. "Anyway, I just wanted to tell you to be careful. I've told the guards to watch your apartment more vigilantly than usual. So if you notice a lot of cops hanging around, you'll know why."

"Okay. Thanks." She frowned. "Do you think it's people from Mercuria?"

"I'm sure of it. No one else has a grudge against me at the moment. At least, no one that I know of."

"Are you still going to the pizza party?"

"Sure."

"Good. What are you wearing?"

"Kayla! I'm not a girl. Who cares what I wear?"

"No, I mean…I forgot to give you back your denim jacket. I left it in the closet at the office. Remind me later to give it back to you."

"I have another one."

"Oh. Hey, I guess you really do like them, don't you?"

He ignored that and when he spoke

again, his voice was lower, almost husky, with a feeling she didn't want to name.

"Hey. I miss you."

Her heart gave a lurch. "No, you don't. You just saw me an hour ago."

"I know. But I still miss you."

"Max, don't. You can't…"

"I know. But I still miss you. Can't help it. See you tomorrow. Good night, Kayla."

"Good night, Max." She closed her eyes to stop the tears that were suddenly threatening. "Happy pizza."

They met for breakfast at nine. She flushed when she saw him waiting for her in the little crepe café. She couldn't help it. All that crazy kissing had made her jumpy for hours.

But he didn't seem to remember it. He had a lot to tell her about his pizza party with his brothers the night before. He'd obviously had a pretty good time, though he wasn't ready to call it that.

"It was okay," he said slowly as he savored the hot cup of coffee the waitress had served him. "I still don't feel really comfortable with them, but they are a great group. I like them all."

And then he went on to tell her in minute detail everything everyone had said. She smiled, listening to him, slowly picking at her blueberry crepe. Could it be that he was beginning to feel a little better about being here?

He had an omelet and a brioche, but he looked tired. And then he yawned.

She frowned. "Didn't you get enough sleep last night?"

He hesitated, looking a bit chagrined. "Actually, no. On my way back from the pizza party I met an old flying buddy I hadn't seen for a while. We went and had a few drinks and…"

She bit back the words that came to mind, but he read her thoughts in her eyes.

"I know, I know. I'm supposed to be learning to be royal, not carousing with old friends." He glowered at her. "The royal life is looking about as appealing as a term in prison."

"It's not that bad," she said, smiling at his funny face. "Royals go out with friends all the time. In fact, some even get in a lot of trouble all the time. Just read the tabloids. But…"

"Kayla, I know what you're worrying about. We're back to the need for me to grow up. I know. I'm working on it."

"I know." She made a face. "I don't mean to be your constant scold. That's not much fun for either of us. And you deserve to have fun." She gave him a silly grin that just oozed affection. How could she help it? She adored him and adored the way he told her what he was thinking all the time. There was very little about Max that was inscrutable.

And then she sobered. "Just don't forget how serious these times are. The war may be officially over, but there is more work to do. This truce with the Granvillis is going to lead to us taking over their area soon and who knows how that will go?"

He looked at her carefully. "You're sure of that, are you?"

"Of the Granvillis surrendering? Everyone says it's about to happen."

He raised his eyebrows. "Funny thing. This old flying buddy I met last night? He has some ties to the Granvillis and he thinks they are getting ready for a new surge."

Her heart sank. "Oh, no."

"He seems to think they're getting some international help they didn't have before."

She shook her head, knowing how terrible it would be if the war heated up again. "You'd better tell Monte," she said anxiously.

He looked away and shrugged. "I might," he said slowly. "I've got to think it over first."

"What?" The very thought that he might hesitate to tell his brother and king something that might be vital to national security floored her.

He glanced back, looking defensive. "It was a private conversation. Just talking with a friend. I can't back any of it up. I'm not sure if he was on the level or just trying to recruit me."

"Recruit you!"

He nodded. "They need flyers." He looked at her, hard. "That's what I do, Kayla. I'm a flyer. It's what I love. I told him I'd think about it."

"But..." She bit her tongue and turned

away, horrified. Didn't he see that doing something like that would be tantamount to treason? She had to find a way to make him understand that he was now a part of the heart and soul of the Ambrian people, and of this royal family. Their destiny was his destiny. All the rest would flow from that.

Turning back, she looked at him, so handsome, so rebellious. She thought of Eddie. He'd been the kind of man who always did the right thing without effort. He was never tortured by doubts the way Max was. But he'd loved the vulnerability in Max as much as she did, and Eddie's own certainty was part of what drew Max to him, as she knew well. Two men, so different, yet both such quality guys. Max just didn't know the extent of his virtue yet. But he would work it out. She had faith in him.

"Max, you're representing the DeAngelis royal family now," she said quietly. "And the nation of Ambria. That has to be your highest priority."

He gave her a skeptical look and the corner of his mouth jerked down. She sighed, thinking about what she would say to him if only she could.

Max, you didn't really grow up here. You have love of country in your blood, but not in your experience. You need both in order to understand what the others take for granted. You will. But you need to be introduced first. How am I going to make sure that happens?

She ached to say those things, but she knew he wasn't ready to hear that right now. He was still feeling resentful.

"No matter what, I won't be a spy," he said, turning to look into her eyes. His jaw-line hardened. "I won't rat on my flying buddies."

She was so tempted to launch into a lecture on duty and patriotism and how those things had to come first, but she stopped herself. She was acting enough like a schoolmarm to turn Max from a best friend into an enemy. She had to learn a few things herself—things about when to hold 'em and when to fold 'em. So she bit her tongue and smiled brightly instead. After all, they were still trying to convince him that he should stay.

She knew one thing. Everyone who came in contact with him wanted him to hang around. But he was so bored with the whole thought of being a prince. She was afraid one of the other offers that kept pouring in would tempt him and he'd be gone.

CHAPTER EIGHT

HALF an hour later, Kayla and Max were taking the elevator down to the main floor, where the gymnasium was located. The gym had a marquee, like an old-fashioned movie theater, and today it was advertising a basketball game that night. But as they walked in, half of the pictures posted in the display boxes had to do with minor sports and most of those were fencing.

"Have you ever studied fencing?" Kayla asked him as they entered the cavernous room. All the princes had been trained and Max would have to learn as well.

"Never." He pretended to wield an imaginary foil. "We didn't do much of that in the crowd I ran with."

"Well, take a good look," she said with a sweep of her hand. "Because you're going to have to learn."

"This lame stuff?" He looked down over the edge of the railing and suddenly hoped his voice hadn't carried that far. Down below were numerous men in white clothing, holding very slender swords.

"Why don't you put on a suit and go in and give it a try? It might just open your eyes." She snickered. "Or kill you."

He gave her a baleful look, but before he could make a rejoinder, someone hailed him from the floor.

"Hey, Max. Come on down here and give me some competition." The fencer pulled up his mask and slashed the air with his foil.

Max laughed, realizing it was his brother Joe. "I don't know one end of a sword from another. I'd probably end up stabbing myself," he called down.

"I was just like you a few months ago," Joe said. "Hey, I spent most of my growing up years on a surfboard in California. What did I know about these ancient ritualistic sports?" He grinned. "But I learned. And it's a lot of fun, actually. Gives you a good workout, too. We'll have to get you set up with lessons."

"Cool," Max said back. "If a surfer boy can learn, I guess a seat-of-the-pants flyer can."

"Absolutely."

"Though I don't know if I can fit it in," Max added, teasing Kayla, though he was still talking to Joe. "I'm real busy learning how to be a prince, you know."

"You have somebody teaching you?" Joe cried. "Hey, how do I get in on that gig?"

"I'll tell Pellea you're interested," Kayla told him with a laugh.

"Do that." He saluted them both. "See you later," he added as he pulled his mask back down and took the ready position.

"He doesn't need any lessons," Max said in admiration. "Look at him."

She did, then she turned back, eyes sparkling. "Max, you ought to look at yourself. You look just as good as he does. It's only a matter of time until you have the confidence to carry it off without a waver."

"Sure," he muttered out of the corner of his mouth. "Whatever you say, teacher lady. I'm here to learn."

Next stop was at the tailor. Mr. Nanvone's father had been the royal tailor thirty years before, and now his son had taken over. Max was less enthusiastic about this visit.

"Why don't we just wait awhile and see if we're really going to need formal wear and all that stuff?" he suggested as they reached the shop. Mannequins in tuxedos lined the show windows. "After all…"

Just then a smartly dressed man emerged from the shop doorway. It took a double take for Max to realize it was another of his brothers.

"Max," Mykal said jovially. "Come to get your fancy formal wear ordered?"

Max made a face. "Unfortunately, it does seem to be the goal here."

Mykal laughed. "We all have to do it. You want to play, you've got to wear the gear."

Max looked him over and blurted out, "What made you decide?"

Mykal looked wary. "Decide what?"

Max shrugged. "Whether you wanted to play or not."

They stared at each other for a long moment and then a grin broke through Mykal's reserve. "So you're still at that stage, are you? Wondering if it's all worth it." He patted him on the shoulder. "Been there, done that. And as you see, I'm still here."

He gave Kayla a wide smile, winked, then turned back to Max.

"Listen, come see me one of these days. We'll talk." And he was off.

Max watched him go, still favoring one side of his body over the other. Max sighed and then turned and followed Kayla into the tailor shop.

"I guess that motorcycle accident really did a number on him, didn't it?" Max murmured to her.

"Yes. He almost died. He had shrapnel in his back, very close to his spine, and they didn't want to operate because of that. But Mykal decided he would take any chance to be whole again, so he insisted on surgery."

Max nodded. "Brave guy." He squared his shoulders. "If he can do this, so can I. Where's the man with the measuring tape?"

Kayla laughed as Mr. Nanvone instantly appeared from behind the curtain barrier into the back room, a measuring tape in his hand.

His session didn't last very long, but by the time the measuring and other necessary particulars were finished, he seemed exhausted.

"The questions were the worst," he told her as they left the shop. "'Which do you prefer,'" he mimicked, copying the tailor's accent, "'ostrich- or pearl-gray, teal or military green, oxford or gold-ore brown.' Too many decisions!"

"Hold it," Kayla said, reaching for her phone. "There's a message from Pellea." She read it quickly. "She wants us to come in right away. They've had a response from Mercuria."

Her gaze met his and he reached out and took her by the hand.

"Let's go."

But as they walked toward the elevator, Max's mood grew more somber.

"I've got a bad feeling about this."

Kayla looked up at him, curious. "What do you expect to go wrong? Things like this usually go on forever. We send our ambassador, they send theirs, they talk, they negotiate, they go back to their respective corners and it all starts again. You hardly ever see anything actually resolved."

He considered her description as they got onto the elevator and punched in the right floor. "I'd feel better if I knew what that historical artifact they think I took was. I mean, one person's historical artifact could be another person's used piece of trash. I wish I had some idea of what we're looking for."

Pellea's face wasn't giving away any clues as they walked into the office.

"Thank you for getting here so quickly," she began. "I feel like things are escalating and I don't want them to spin out of control."

"Of course not," Kayla agreed. "What have you heard?"

The queen waited while they took chairs, then continued. "I think I explained to you how the charges were addressed by our ambassador. He handed our letter to King Juomo personally. Here is the king's response."

She held up a large, embossed and very official-looking document.

"'The plane and the horse are nothing to

us. We are willing to let them go. The artifact is everything. We must have it back. There is only one way we will accept its return. Max Arragen must himself bring it back to Helgium Castle and offer it by hand to the Princess Nadine. No other method will suffice.'"

Pellea looked up and cocked her head in Max's direction. "Princess Nadine?" she said questioningly. "A new element has been added. Care to elaborate?"

Max sighed and looked guilty. "I should have told you about Princess Nadine."

Pellea's eyes flashed. "Yes, you should have."

Quickly he told her the same thing he had told Kayla, explaining how crazy this was, at least in his opinion. "She's just a teenaged girl with a teenaged crush. Nothing more."

"A teenaged girl with the power to start a war." Pellea glared at him. "And possibly have you executed."

Executed. That was an ugly and very serious word. Everyone in the room seemed to reverberate to the vibes coming off just the sound of it for a moment.

Pellea was the first to break out of the spell. "All right, here's the rest. 'You have only three days left to comply with our demands. We are preparing for an invasion.'" She looked out at the others. "An invasion. The man is crazy, but then, those who invade other countries often are."

There was a long silence, and then Max looked up.

"Why don't I go? They can't hold this whole country responsible for me if I'm not here and haven't officially been made a part of the royal court. Just call me the black sheep, the one you can't control, the one you can do nothing about. They can't expect you to pay for my crimes."

"Impossible. You are a prince of Ambria. We can't let you go."

He looked down again, then up. "You know, I didn't do anything," he said softly to Pellea.

She half smiled. "Max, if I thought you had done anything at all with a fifteen-year-old girl, we wouldn't even be talking here anymore."

He looked relieved. "Of course not."

Kayla moved restlessly. "I think you

should tell the queen about what happened to your rooms last night."

Pellea turned a questioning face Max's way. "Yes?"

"When I got in late last evening, I found my apartment ransacked. I think it was probably Mercurians after that darn artifact, whatever it may be."

"Interesting." She frowned. "Why weren't you better guarded?"

He shrugged. "I've talked to the captain of the guard. I think conditions will improve."

"Good." She frowned again as he told her the situation and what had been done to his things.

"You're sure nothing was taken?"

"As far as I can tell."

"And you think it was the Mercurians?"

He nodded. "I'm sure of it."

"Well, I guess we all had better be on our guard," Pellea warned. "Those darn Mercurians."

"Mercurians!"

That was the first thing Kayla thought when she opened the door to her own apartment later that afternoon. Everything looked normal at first, but she could tell. She had the distinct feeling that things were different. Strangers had been in her place. Nothing seemed to be missing. But there was a sense of invasion. Her personal space had been violated. She was sure of it.

She called Max right away.

"They tried hard to put everything back just the way it was," she said. "But I can tell. These creepy people have been all through my things. Ugh!"

"Did you call the security guards?"

"No." She felt a bit abashed. "I called you."

"I'll call them. And I'll be there in a few minutes."

"Oh, I don't want to bother you, Max. I know you have things to do."

"I'm coming over and I'm bringing my toothbrush and jammies."

"What? You can't stay here."

"Try and stop me."

She had to laugh after she hung up. He did have a way about him. But amusement fled when the security people arrived and claimed they couldn't find any evidence of a break in.

"How can you be sure your things were moved? Suppose you moved them yourself and forgot you did it?"

She had a feeling they were snickering at her behind her back, but they got serious when Max arrived. He wasn't pleased that they hadn't been watching her apartment more carefully, as he'd requested. They promised to be more vigilant.

"You see, you don't have to stay," she told him once they'd gone. "I'll be okay."

"Yes, you'll be fine. Because I will be here with you."

"Really?" She gave him an exasperated look. "And how long do you plan to stay here?"

"Until the Mercurians stop looking for the artifact."

She made a face at him. "That could take a long, long time."

"Look, this is just for tonight. We'll deal with the rest of our lives later. Okay?"

He had a few errands to run but he was back an hour later. He'd been looking forward to his night with Kayla with mixed feelings. It would be a delight to be with her, even if the mood was platonic, but he knew that Teddy probably came with the package. When he arrived at the door and glanced around the room, sure enough, there was the kid, sitting in a little plastic chair and playing with a stuffed dinosaur.

He wanted to like Teddy. The child was beautiful with huge blue eyes and a head of dark bronze curls. He looked adorable. But the kid hated him. He really seemed to have something against him. But that wasn't fair. He was only a baby. Babies didn't hate. Did they? They wanted what they wanted the minute they wanted it. Teddy wanted his mama and didn't want to share her with some strange man. Who could blame him?

Sure. He grinned to himself. That was all it was. He had to stop letting his imagination run away with him.

He'd thought about this ahead of time. He knew what he had to do. He went right up to the child. "Hi, Teddy," he said in a friendly manner. "What's that you've got there? A tyrannosaurus?"

The blue eyes glanced up at him and shot back down to stare at his toy.

There you go, he thought. *The kid hates me.*

He was at a loss. He'd never had any experience with children this age and he had no idea how to deal with them. He looked up at Kayla for help.

She stepped forward and he thought she seemed a little nervous. "Teddy, can you say 'hi' to Prince Max?"

Obviously not. Teddy's lower lip came out and he stared very hard at his dinosaur.

"All right, we'll work on that later," she said with forced cheer. "But you're going to have to learn to be polite to visitors."

"Leave him alone," Max murmured to the side. "Let him get used to me." As if he knew the secrets to popularity with the Rugrat crowd.

She produced a batch of oven-fried chicken that was as good as anything the colonel made, along with crispy biscuits and a nice green salad. Even Teddy took a few bites. She'd also made some rubbery green gelatin squares that were so tough, they could play catch with them. Once he saw those, Teddy suddenly had an appetite. He came over to watch, hanging on his mother's leg and leaning his head on her knee, and when Max tossed a square into the air and caught it with his mouth, Teddy couldn't help it—he just had to laugh.

When it was time for bed, Teddy went down fairly easily.

"Help me tuck him in," Kayla urged.

"Why?"

She gave him a look and he reluctantly followed her into the bedroom. When Teddy saw Max, he hid his face in the covers.

"You see," Max whispered to her. "He doesn't want me to be here when you tuck him in."

"He's a child," she muttered back. "You're a grown-up. You're the one in charge of the situation. Don't let him con you."

So he helped tuck Teddy in. But the kid still seemed to hate him. He wasn't sure why that should be—or why he cared. He'd known other kids who didn't seem to adore him and it had never bothered him before. Maybe it was the fact that he'd expected to have instant rapport with Eddie's boy. That hadn't happened.

He came out into the kitchen and helped her with the dishes, taking a towel and drying them as she put them up on the counter, sparkling clean. They talked about old times and laughed about old stories. And Kayla realized that Max was really her only link to Eddie, physical or emotional. The memories were all in his head, like they were in her heart. Was that what drew her to him so strongly? Was that what made her feel something very close to love whenever she looked into his eyes?

No. It was more than that. Much more. If only she could pin down exactly what it was.

She got him a beer and she made herself a cup of hot tea and they sat on the couch and talked softly.

She stretched and smiled at him. "You know what? In this very moment, in spite of everything, I'm very happy."

"Why?"

"Because you're here. And because you seem to be at peace in a way. Not quite as tense and restless as you usually are."

She was right. It was good being with her this way. She made him happy, too. He looked at her pretty face, her soft brown eyes, her beautiful lips and he felt an ache where his heart should be.

"You need to be kissed," he murmured, looking at her mouth a bit hungrily.

She shook her head and began to appear wary. "No, I don't."

"Yes, you do." Reaching out, he touched her chin, then curled his hand around her jawline. "Or maybe I should say, I need to kiss you. That might be more honest."

Searching into his deep, mysterious eyes, she laughed softly. His hand felt so warm on her skin and his breath was even warmer on her face. She needed to pull away, let him know she couldn't let him keep the promise that was smoldering in his eyes. But somehow, that just wasn't happening.

"You don't need to kiss me," she said. "Kisses are for lovers. We're not going to do that."

A slight frown creased his brow. "You don't get it. I do need to kiss you. And you need to kiss me. Just me and you. And nothing about Eddie."

She closed her eyes for a moment, and then she looked into his again with a tiny, sad smile.

"I don't want you to do anything that you'll regret," she told him, half joking.

He frowned. "What is it that you regret?"

She shook her head, letting her sleek blond hair brush against his hand. "I don't regret anything. There was a time when I did. But I got over that quickly enough." Turning her face, she caught the palm of his hand against her lips and put a kiss there. "One look into my baby's eyes, and regrets faded away," she added softly.

He stared at her and a look of pain flashed in his eyes. "Kayla…"

"Hush." She put a finger to his lips. "Just kiss me."

And he did.

His mouth was hot and hard on hers and she moaned low in her throat, a deep, primal sound of pleasure. She'd been so lonely for so long, to feel his arms around her, to feel the joy of his true affection, seemed to bring her out of a long sleep and into the sunlight. Their tongues met, caressed, tangled, then seemed to meld together into one smoldering focus of heat and her whole body was ready to burst into flames.

"Oh!" she cried, pulling away and staring at him. "Oh, my gosh, Max. We can't even kiss without setting the world on fire. What the heck?"

He lay back against the pillows on the couch and started to laugh. She batted at him, then started to laugh as well, falling on him and holding him close as they both enjoyed the moment.

"Just let me hold you," he murmured, face buried in her hair. "I just want to feel you against me."

She nodded. "Me, too." And then she sighed. It took a while for her body to calm down. She knew in her heart that they would make love again and it would be soon. But not now. For now, this was enough. In fact, it was a certain brand of heaven.

A sound from Teddy's room made her get up to check on him. She looked down at her sleeping child and her heart was so full, for a moment, she couldn't breathe. She came out with a new determination. It was time.

"Max, we have to talk about it."

He looked up, startled at her tone. "Talk about what?"

"That night. That night after Eddie died."

His heart began to pound in his chest. "No. We don't have anything to talk about." His words were defensive and so was his tone. He was scared to talk about it. Anyone could see that.

She gestured for him to follow her. "Come here. I want you to look at this baby."

"No. Kayla…"

Reaching out, she grabbed his arm. "Come here. Look at him. You have to."

He came reluctantly, sure that this would do no good and make no difference. What was the point?

He looked down. Teddy really was a beautiful child. Something was fluttering in his chest.

"Look at him," she was saying softly, almost whispering. "His face is so sweet when he's asleep. Those big round cheeks." She turned to look at him. "If his eyes were open, you would see how blue they are."

"Kayla." He winced.

"He's an adorable, sweet little boy. And you're not letting him into your heart."

He closed his eyes, searching for an inner strength he wasn't sure he was going to find.

"Is he mine?" His voice was tortured, vibrating with pain.

"You know the answer."

He closed his eyes again and turned away, pushing his way back out to the living room. She followed, wondering if he'd felt what she wanted him to feel.

"How could we have done that, Kayla?" he was muttering angrily. "How could we have betrayed Eddie like that?"

"At the time we did it, it seemed like a sacrament. A tribute. An homage to his life. It was only later, in the sober light of day, that it seemed like a betrayal."

He nodded. "I remember it well."

Suddenly she turned on him. She threw a pillow at him and then cried fiercely, "Max, don't you dare regret it! Don't you dare!"

"Kayla…"

"That night, after we found out there was no hope of finding Eddie alive, we were in shock. The pain was so great—do you remember? We turned to each other to stem it. We told ourselves we were celebrating his life, but we were really trying to pay back the fates for what they'd done to us... to Eddie."

He nodded but he didn't say a word.

"All we could do was cry and hold on to each other. And somehow, we ended up doing something we never meant to do. But it happened." She pulled on his arm. "Don't deny it! It happened."

He turned his head away.

"A miracle came out of that, despite everything. My sweet baby. Our sweet baby. Don't you dare deny that."

Max took a deep breath and turned back to look her full in her tearstained face.

"No. I won't deny it. But I do regret it."

He took her in his arms and she cried and cried.

It was a few hours later. Max was asleep on the couch. He raised his head, wondering what he'd heard, and then he realized it was Kayla. She was singing softly to her baby. He listened, staying very still. There was something in that voice, something in the love she had for her child, that gave him chills. It touched him like nothing else and tears came to his eyes, stinging.

He'd never thought it would happen. He was the perennial bachelor. He was famous for it. No woman had ever been able to make her way through that tough shield of reality and reach his heart. Only Kayla had. And yet, he couldn't get around it. To love her was a betrayal of Eddie.

CHAPTER NINE

"LISTEN," Max said as he left in the morning. "I won't be able to stay with you tonight. Can you make arrangements to stay with Caroline?"

"Maybe." Kayla knew she sounded defensive, but that was how she felt. She knew he was upset, that things said and done from the night before had thrown him off again, and she resented it. "We'll see."

He hesitated, as though he wanted to argue with her, but then thought better of it. "Okay," he said. "I'll call you later."

And he was gone. She stared at the door as it closed, a lump in her throat. He was regretting again. She was losing him.

She fixed breakfast for Teddy and took him to her sister's, then hurried on to the office. Pellea was on a tear, racing from one project to another, barking out orders and ideas, and Kayla didn't have time to find out what had been decided as a response to the Mercurians. And then, suddenly, Max was back and he didn't have the scowl he'd had that morning.

"Look at this," he said, his blue eyes sparkling with new energy. "Research has come up with a picture of the artifact."

He had a thick book with beautiful photographic illustrations, and there was a huge picture of the item in question. They gathered around and stared at it and for a few minutes, no one said a word.

"Wow," Pellea said at last. "No wonder they want it back."

The historical artifact was a beautiful medallion on a thick gold chain. The background was encrusted with rubies and emeralds and the centerpiece was a huge, elongated, multifaceted diamond. It took a moment or two to realize that the gems formed a picture of a green field and a tree with rubies as apples. The diamond in the center seemed to represent a huge waterfall. On the next page, the image of the backside showed a date almost four centuries old and the name Mercuria.

"Wow," Kayla breathed, echoing the queen. "I've never seen anything so gorgeous."

"And probably worth more than ten small countries thrown together," Pellea said. "Max, did you ever have it in your possession?"

"Are you kidding? Do you think I could have forgotten something like this? Or mislaid it? I've never seen this before. And I damn well know I never held it in my hand."

They looked at each other.

"How about this?" Max asked after a moment of silence. "Do we have some sort of video communication system set up with King Juomo? If so, I could tell him face-to-face that I didn't take this and don't have it, without actually going there."

Pellea nodded. "We've got the capability. Heck, I could do it from my notebook. But as I understand it, it will take some time to set up the official, royal version that they can use, too," she said. "I'll try to have the technicians on it right away."

Then she frowned. "In the meantime, you be careful. People have been known to do some ugly things to get their hands on a piece of jewelry like that."

"Don't worry. I've got my eyes open." He gave a simple bow to the queen and a faint smile to Kayla, and then he was out the door.

Kayla was glad to know he was now certain he had not taken the artifact, but she was not so happy with his new dismissive attitude. She was mulling over how to respond to it when Pellea walked up and leaned on her desk with both hands.

"What are we going to do about Max?" she said in a quiet voice, meant to stay clear of any eavesdroppers.

Kayla was startled. "Why? What's wrong?"

"Nothing new. Just the usual. I'm still worried about his lack of commitment to becoming a prince. His heart isn't in it. Not yet."

She only hesitated a moment before taking the plunge. "I'm afraid you're right. At least, in part. I think he's coming around, but it's going to take some time."

Pellea sighed. "The others seemed to be

able to make the adjustment to royal status quickly and easily. I don't know if he's just too rigid in his ways or what. I'm really afraid that he might not be able to do it." She shook her head, looking worried. "There's something wild and free in him. Something that resists rules and borders. I'm not sure he'll be able to stay."

Kayla knew the queen was emotionally invested in Max's success, still, she was surprised to see she had tears in her eyes. Kayla reached for her hand and held it with genuine affection.

"Oh, Pellea, don't give up on him."

"Oh, I can't. We need him. The family won't be whole without him. Like a family portrait with one face cut out. Can you imagine? Impossible! It will kill Monte if he doesn't stay. Now that the war is basically won, now that Leonardo Granvilli is dead, he has such plans for this country."

"I'm sure he'll stay," she said, wishing she could sound more convincing. But that was hard when she wasn't sure what she was saying was true. "He just needs seasoning."

Pellea dried her eyes and gave Kayla a

watery smile. "I still have hope. I do have one ace in the hole, you know. You see, I have one piece of bait, one promise, one prize that just might keep him here."

Kayla looked innocent. "What is that?"

Pellea laughed. "You!"

"Me? Oh, no, no, no, no."

"Yes, you my dear. It obvious the two of you are in love. Or hadn't you noticed?"

Luckily, a visitor arrived in time to save Kayla from having to answer that. She went back to work, typing as fast as she could, her cheeks hot and rosy. What Pellea was suggesting was insane. She knew Max well enough to know he wasn't husband material. He wasn't even father material. He was a wild man. And after last night, she was afraid there was no hope of anything taming him.

Kayla sent a message asking Max to come for dinner, and to her surprise, he showed up, despite the fact that he hadn't contacted her all day. It was funny how lonely that had made her. In just a few days she'd become used to hearing from him constantly and she missed it when it wasn't there. She served meat loaf and mashed potatoes and he had two helpings. Though he started out seeming a bit distant, he soon warmed up as he told her about talking to the king of Mercuria on the video phone connection.

"We weren't exactly buddies when I was working on organizing the air force last year," he said. "But we did work together often and we got along well. Unfortunately, he doesn't seem to remember all that."

"What did he say?"

"He insists I have the artifact. He says he has proof."

"Proof? What sort of proof?"

Max hesitated. Then he made a wry, apologetic face and told her the truth. "He says that Princess Nadine gave it to me personally when she knew I was leaving. She supposedly gave it to me so that it would bring me back to her." He looked at a loss. "Believe me, I barely ever spoke to the girl. And she never gave me anything. I was hardly ever that close to her."

Kayla nodded, thinking hard. She had no doubt at all that Max was telling the truth. But how could the princess have thought she was giving it to him when she wasn't at all? And where was it now?

Teddy was playing about their feet as they finished their dinner. He had a large, open plastic bus and a small plastic horse and he was very intent on making the horse drive the bus. It seemed to make perfect sense to him that a horse would be driving. But at one point the horse fell out and the bus ran right over him.

Teddy gasped. Max reacted without thinking, reaching down to save the horse. "Poor little horsey," he said, pretending to make the animal neigh back at him. "The horsey wants to go back in the bus," he told Teddy, as though he'd understood the neigh. "Here." He put him back in the driver's seat.

Teddy stared up at him, eyes wide. Then, suddenly, he grinned right up at Max. It was a bright grin, a complete grin, full of joy, no holds barred. Max's heart almost stopped. He'd never known. No one had ever told him what a baby's smile could do. It knocked him out and then some. He felt something explode in his chest and realized it was his heart starting up again.

Teddy had already forgotten the moment and gone back to playing with the bus. Max turned and looked at Kayla. She smiled at him.

"Wonderful, isn't it?" she murmured.

She understood. He didn't have to say anything and she understood. He glanced back at Teddy, at his own sweet baby. A baby who didn't hate him after all. He could hardly breathe, he was so happy.

They talked softly for a while longer, and the euphoria faded. He still didn't feel right about how Teddy had come to be. It had been wrong and he feared he would have to pay for that wrong, somehow.

"Are you okay?" Kayla asked.

He looked at her. She was so beautiful with the lamplight making a halo behind her beautiful hair. He wanted her—wanted her in his life and in his bed and in his dreams. Wanted her with an ache that throbbed inside and almost made him crazy. But he wasn't ready to tell her so. He had so many things to think about and he was having trouble keeping it all straight.

He might leave. Just go. He'd done it before. In fact, it was the way he normally operated. Stay in one place as long as it pleased him, then, when things got tough, just go. He might do it again. He didn't want it to happen. He was trying, really trying to change his ways, to find meaning in life and stick to it. But he knew himself well enough to know it might not work that way. He might just go.

He got up to leave. He had to go out on his own and figure out what was in his head and in his heart.

"Thanks for the great dinner," he told her. "Promise me you'll stay with Caroline tonight."

"I will. As soon as you're gone, we'll go over there." She searched his eyes. "Will I see you tomorrow?"

He avoided meeting her gaze. "I don't know. I've got a lot to think about. I may go off on my own for a while." He shrugged. "And I have to decide what to do about Mercuria. I can't let them attack this country." He shook his head, looking bemused. "What a concept, huh? Like a comic opera. But they are just crazy enough, they might do it."

Kayla went up to say goodbye, then went

on tiptoes and kissed him on the lips, surprising him. "I love you," she told him.

Everything in him cried out for him to take her in his arms and give her what she deserved, but he held back. He held her shoulders and felt her lovely rounded flesh, so warm, so inviting. But he held back. She didn't mean that she was in love with him. She loved him. She had always loved him, just as he'd loved Eddie. They had all loved each other. But that didn't mean they were in love. Was he in love with her? That was just one more question he had to deal with.

He had to figure this out.

"Goodbye. I'll call you."

She nodded and watched him go, then turned to her son.

"No crying," she told herself sternly. "We have things we have to do."

She packed Teddy's bag and then went into the closet to get some things of her own to take along to Caroline's. She'd finally brought the denim jacket back from the office and then she'd forgotten to give it to him again. Even worse, it had slipped off the hanger and lay on the floor. She picked it up and pressed it to her face, reveling in the scent that reminded her of Max. Then she put it back on the hanger, noting that it was an awfully heavy jacket. And she finished packing and grabbed her son and headed out to her sister's apartment.

The next day was unusually busy and different from their normal routine. In the morning, there was a meeting Pellea had set up that she wanted all the princes—and Princess Kim—to attend.

"I'd like all of the new princes to meet with the prime minister," she told Kayla that morning, "and begin to get an idea of what they need to study about our history and foreign policy matters. They need to begin developing what their duties will be. That, of course, will depend a lot on each one's individual skills and talents and how they can be used to best serve this country."

Pellea's face was quite serious, as though she'd given this a lot of thought. "Some of them still don't realize that they can't keep up the sort of lifestyle they are used to if they want to be serious about this royalty business."

"Yes, I agree with you," Kayla said softly, wondering if she mainly had Max in mind.

Pellea went on, completely filled with her own sense of purpose. "When you take on this way of living, you are taking on a responsibility for the lives, happiness and well-being of your people. And that means everybody in this castle, everybody on the royal side of the island, and even those rebels still siding with the Granvillis. Because eventually we'll win them over, too, and the kingdom will be united again."

Kayla nodded. "Have you told them all where and when?" she asked, wondering if she ought to give Max a call to remind him.

"Yes. Ten o'clock in the blue meeting room. And then, of course, we have the picnic luncheon for the French foreign minister and his family, out on the south lawn. Practically everyone in the castle will be coming to that one. Free food does tend to gather a crowd."

The phone began to ring and the queen was soon engrossed in one conversation after another. Meanwhile, Kayla tried to get hold of Max. She called, she sent messages, she even emailed him, but there was no response. As time went by, she began to be concerned, wondering what could have happened to him. She knew he'd planned to go off on his own for a while to think things over, but surely he was checking his messages.

Unless…

Unless he'd left the island. Unless he'd decided just to go. Her heart raced and she got a sick feeling in the pit of her stomach.

"All right, I'm off to the prime minister's meeting with the princes. I'm sure you'll be able to handle things while I'm gone. I'll go straight to the picnic from there. And don't you forget to come to that. Afterward, we'll work on the response to Mercuria."

Kayla nodded, wondering how long it would be before she got a panicked call from the meeting telling her to find Max. When the hour went by without that call, she began to relax. Surely Pellea would have called her if he hadn't shown up. Maybe everything was okay. Maybe she was letting her imagination run away with her.

And maybe she would go to the picnic luncheon after all. Max might even be there. She put away her work and hurried over to the other side of the castle, glad she'd worn dark slacks and a crisp white shirt rather than her usual skirt and sweater. She was dressed for a picnic.

She came out on an upper level and looked down. From where she was standing, she could see the royal platform. And there were Pellea and King Monte and all the princes. All the princes except one. No Max.

Her heart fell. Where could he be? She bit her lip and tried to calm down. There was no point running around like a headless chicken. She had to be logical. The first place to look would be at his rooms.

Going back quickly through the halls, she made her way there in ten minutes. The usual guard was gone and when she knocked, no one answered.

Strike one. Where could she try next? Okay, he'd said he was going off on his own to think. He'd shown her his favorite place to do that, the flat rock by the stream. There was a balcony that looked right down over that area. That would provide the quickest access. She raced toward it.

There was an eerie feeling in this side of the castle today. The usually bustling halls were empty. Everyone was at the picnic. Kayla tried to calm herself down, but she was feeling a bit spooked.

Finally, out of breath, she reached the balcony, and with it, a sense of instant calm. She leaned out over the balcony railing, breathing in the fresh air and reveling in the feeling of freedom. White clouds scudded across a china blue sky. It was a beautiful day and a beautiful setting. Looking down, she didn't see Max, but she did see a glorious view of the countryside, and she knew Max was down there somewhere. Surely he would begin to feel better about everything after a few hours walking about the grounds. She knew she would. She leaned out a bit farther and searched the hills and valleys for a sign of him.

All in all, she was glad she had brought her baby here to the castle. She had a good job and a nice place to live. No complaints. The only element lacking was a daddy for her baby. Other than that, things were coming up roses.

Finally, a movement caught her eye, but it came from right below where she was standing. Two men were struggling with a large push cart. From her vantage point, she could see a large white van parked in a stretch of trees toward the main road. It looked like they were headed that way. But why not bring the van down to the castle and load their cargo in a convenient place? Only one reason she could think of. They were doing something illegal.

And that was certainly the feeling you got from watching them. Their movements were a little too quick, and a lot too furtive. Funny. What could they be transporting that they knew they shouldn't be? Equipment they'd stolen? Machinery they'd found in a storeroom? The entire contents of someone's living room?

That reminded her of the way her place had been manhandled and Max's ransacked. She looked at the men more carefully. Was there anything about them that could be said to seem Mercurian? Not really. They looked like normal workmen. But still…

A siren sounded, making her jump. Sirens were not unusual. There seemed to be a fire drill every week, mostly because of the legacy of the castle burning during the Granvilli rebellion. But this was no drill, not in the middle of a state picnic luncheon. She frowned and looked down at the workmen. The siren seemed to have panicked them. They were running now, pushing at each other and shouting. The pushcart hit a rock and nearly overturned. The canvas cover came off and their cargo was revealed. There was a man lying inside, scrunched into a curled-up position. The man was either dead or unconscious, and he looked very much like Max.

She gasped. The cover was quickly restored, but she knew what she'd seen. Could this be the Mercurians? They looked so guilty. Had they grabbed Max? She wasn't at all sure that was who she'd seen, but still, just the possibility threw her for a loop.

Her heart was pounding like a drum in her own ears. Her hands were shaking so hard, she could barely use her mobile to call security. It rang and rang.

"Come on!" she muttered, nearly crazy.

And finally someone answered.

"Quick," she cried. "This is Kayla Mandrake. I've just seen two men kidnapping someone. I think it might be Prince Max."

"No, can't be," he said. "The princes are all at the picnic. I just saw them there."

"Did you see Max?"

He hesitated. "He's the new one, right? I don't think I've ever seen him, so…"

"Please, please, come quickly. They're going to get away!"

"Lady, listen, do you hear that siren? We're shorthanded right now. We've got that darn picnic and now everyone else is out responding to the fire in the library area. There's no one here but me and I can't leave the phone. Listen, call back in about ten minutes. I'll see what I can do then."

"What?"

She couldn't believe it, but she didn't have time to argue. She tried Pellea's number, and then Caroline. Something was wrong; she couldn't get anyone. There was no one to help her. She looked down.

They still hadn't reached the van. Maybe she could catch them herself.

Oh, sure. Catch them and do what? Yell at them a lot? Besides, she would never catch them before they got to the van. And then, who knew where they would go?

But wait. She did know where they would go. What had Max said? She remembered his words— "Mercuria is an hour away," or something like that. An hour away from where? The docks.

The docks! And that wasn't very far. In fact, she knew a shortcut. Caroline and her husband had twin motor scooters that they had used on weekend getaways before their boy was born. She still had a key to Caroline's scooter on her key ring. She could take that scooter and make it across the dunes to the docks before the van got past the traffic signals. There would be officials at the docks. Someone would be there to help her.

She raced down the hall to the stairway. She didn't have time for the elevators. The whole time she ran, she kept looking for someone who might help her, but the halls were empty. She would have to do this herself.

She made her way to the parking garage and found Caroline's scooter. Miraculously, the engine popped on with no trouble, and she was off, dashing for the dunes.

There was a small part of her brain that kept poking her, saying, *What if it is just a body? What if...what if...*

And she pushed it back, saying, *No! They may have said dead or alive, but everything they've done proves they want him alive. So don't even think that!*

She veered off the main road onto a dirt track that cut out about a mile of driving to the docks. The little scooter was racing along and she was feeling very scared, but strangely exhilarated at the same time. She saw the craggy outcropping of the rocky point ahead. That meant the docks were only a few minutes away.

As she came around a curve, the main road was spread out below and she saw the white van. It was turning around. She jammed on her brakes and pulled to a stop.

A man was running from it and another lay on the side of the road. A shot rang out, and then another. Her heart in her throat, she started down the incline, racing to get to the place where the trees stood near the road and she could get a view of the van as it passed without being seen herself.

If her guess were right, that should be Max driving. It looked to her as though he'd overpowered his kidnappers and taken off with their van, but she couldn't be sure. Ditching the scooter behind a small hill, she ran for the edge of the road and made it close enough to see, gasping for breath, just as the van came around the corner.

It was! She could see Max driving. It looked like he had a bloody head wound, but he was driving and as far as she could see, he was alone.

He'd done it! What a guy! Jumping for joy, she yelled and waved her arms, but she was still too far into the trees and he didn't see her.

She had a small, empty feeling when he drove on past and left her there, but she knew it wouldn't be long before she caught up with him again. She turned to run back to her scooter, and that was when she felt the dart go into her neck. She reached to pull it out, but her hands never made it there. In seconds, she was out like a light.

Max had been back at the castle for over an hour and had told everyone his story of being kidnapped by Mercurians. Even King Monte had come by to hear it personally. The whole thing seemed crazy, but everyone wanted to hear it.

Max had spent most of the morning out on his flat rock by the little river, thinking his life over and trying to make some important decisions. He knew Pellea wanted him at the prime minister's meeting, and he had come back to the castle for that, but just as he was coming in through the big double doors, someone had shot a tranquilizer dart into his neck and he had collapsed. He'd woken an hour or so later to find himself locked in a storeroom. This time they put him out with a rag soaked in chloroform, and he woke up in the back of the white van on his way to the docks. His hands were tied, but not very well, and he had no trouble working them free. Then he'd bided his time, not letting the two men know he was awake and that his hands were free. Finally he got his chance and he overpowered one of them. The driver pulled over to help his friend and Max threw the first man out and dealt with the second. Then it was a simple matter of grabbing the keys and taking the same transportation back again, minus the kidnappers this time.

"Though one of them did shoot at the van as I drove off," he told his attentive audience. "Luckily, he wasn't much of a shot."

Security at the docks had been alerted but they hadn't found the men.

"I'm calling out the army on this," Monte said with a scowl. "I want someone charged and put behind bars. We have to nip this sort of thing off right away. We can't have criminals running around kidnapping people."

By now, Max had asked where Kayla was a number of times and no one seemed to know. And then a call came in from the dockyard police saying they had found Caroline's abandoned scooter near the road to the docks, and Pellea and Max began to piece together different bits of evidence and get a vague idea of where she might be. Their conclusions were grim.

Once Pellea questioned the security guard who had been on duty that afternoon and found out someone had called in saying Max had been kidnapped, the picture became clearer.

"Kayla obviously saw the kidnappers taking you off and when she couldn't get security to help, she grabbed Caroline's scooter and went after you herself."

Max stared at Pellea, stunned.

"They have her," he said in a low, gravelly voice. "The bastards have her." He turned to look for his keys. "I've got to go."

CHAPTER TEN

"HOLD IT."

Monte held a hand up and stopped Max cold.

"You're not going anywhere."

Max's face darkened rebelliously. Right now he wasn't in the mood to take orders from royals, no matter who they were. But before he had a chance to say anything, Monte continued and explained his position.

"I'm not trying to pull rank on you, Max. But we have to stop and think things through before we act. We need to be sure we are doing the smart thing to get the results that we want and not just more bloodshed. You swimming the channel in a burst of adrenaline, showing up on shore with a knife between your teeth, is just going to get you killed. We can't succeed without a plan."

"What sort of plan?"

"I say we go in at midnight."

"Who's 'we'?"

"All of us royals. The warriors of the DeAngelis regime. We've got a very fast, very slinky boat that can enter areas without making a sound. I'm thinking four of us will take it."

"Four?" Mykal asked the question.

Monte nodded. "Sorry, old man, but I don't think we ought to risk you on this mission. You're not healed yet. We'll use you as a coordinator back home."

Mykal nodded reluctantly.

"Okay, so we've got Joe with his special forces training. And you, Max—you've been in combat. David is the best strategic thinker I know of. And I'm a pretty good leader." He shrugged. "What else do we need?"

"A plan," Max answered, still restless and not sure this was going to work. He liked to work alone. That was what he was used to. And every minute they delayed was a minute more Kayla had to endure whatever they were putting her through.

"A plan would be good," Monte admitted. "That's why we're going to take a few hours to think about it. We'll meet at eleven and go over our thoughts and put something together.

Max stared at him, trying not to let his resentment show. He knew what Monte was saying was smart, but he wanted to go now. He clenched his jaw and kept his opinion to himself. Monte knew what he was doing and he was exhibiting good leadership. He had to let this play out. Still, he ached to go right into their castle and save Kayla. If someone was hurting her, they were going to pay.

"I'm preparing a message for King Juomo and his ministers," Pellea said. "I'm telling the king that this nonsense has to end and that he'll personally pay for anything that happens to Kayla." She took a deep breath and looked around at them all. "You know it is possible that this is just a fringy, rogue element who has masterminded this," she said.

"You think so?" Max challenged her. "You don't think the king sending a poster saying I was wanted dead or alive was a little rogue, a little fringy?"

"Of course it was."

"Yes. The whole Mercurian royal family has been cuckoo for years."

"Which means you can't base your estimates of what they might do on normal reactions. Be ready for anything."

Max couldn't face going back to his room alone and thinking any more. He wanted to take action. It killed him to wait. He had to do something to take his mind off it. So he stopped by Caroline's apartment and asked to see Teddy.

Caroline was worried. He could see it in her face, and when he decided to take Teddy to Kayla's and fix him some dinner himself, she readily agreed, but caught him before he left.

"Are you going to save my sister?" she asked earnestly. "Can you guarantee me that she's going to be okay?"

He took her hand in his and gazed deep

into her eyes. "I guarantee she'll be okay," he said gruffly. "Or I'll die trying to make that happen."

She stared back for a moment, then nodded, satisfied. "Okay," she said. "I'll hold you to that."

"Come on, Teddy," he said, looking at his little boy. "You want to go with me?"

Teddy gave him a steady gaze but didn't look enthused.

"Go with Prince Max, honey," Carolyn said. "I'll bet he could fix you a nice scrambled egg for your dinner." She said as an aside, "He really likes scrambled eggs," and Max nodded, smiling as the little boy got up and came to him.

"I'll bring him back in an hour or so."

He bent down and picked him up and they said goodbye, but Teddy was stiff in his arms until he saw that they were going to his own apartment. Max realized he probably thought he was going to see his mother, so he began talking to him as they entered the room, keeping him occupied as long as possible, and it seemed to work out all right.

They sat on the floor and Max began putting together a set of fat train tracks meant for toddlers, while Teddy pushed the train engine and tried to make train noises. The tracks were going everywhere, and since the door was open to the coat closet, soon they were going there, too.

Max looked at the little boy he was playing with and he couldn't help but smile. This child was his son. And then Teddy looked at him and gave him that beautiful smile again, and he felt it—the connection. Finally. This really was his son. He could feel it now.

He got up to go fix Teddy some scrambled eggs. He couldn't eat anything himself, he was too tied up in knots, but he fed his boy. And then he paced the floor and thought of Kayla.

Suddenly he noticed a flash of light and he turned, puzzled. A sort of reflection was on the wall. He turned again, trying to figure out where it was coming from, and realized Teddy had pushed his toys into the closet and was pretending it was a cave. But something he was playing with had made that fantastic reflection, all dancing, shimmering lights.

He went into the closet and the first thing he noticed was his own denim jacket, lying on the floor. Realizing it must have fallen, he picked it up and put it on a hanger, then looked down at Teddy. The boy had a thick gold chain around his neck and he was playing with the pendant hanging from it. Max frowned and took a closer look, and then his blood began to pound in his veins and his heart did a flip in his chest.

"What the…?"

It was the artifact. He was staring down at a million-dollar diamond and his son was playing with it.

He turned away, struggling for breath. The historical artifact that threatened to ruin his life, the jewel-encrusted icon worth millions, was in the hands of a toddler. He turned back.

"Teddy, Teddy, where did you get that?"

Teddy didn't seem to know, but Max looked at his own denim jacket and realized what must have happened.

"It was in my jacket all this time," he muttered in hazy wonder. "And it took Teddy to find it."

And Teddy didn't want to give it up.

"Sorry, kid," he told him. "I've got to take this from you. I can't let it out of my possession again. Lives may depend on it."

Looking at it, he was sure this was what the king of Mercuria wanted. He didn't want Kayla. He didn't even want Max. This was basically the crown jewels of the nation and he wanted his treasure back.

How had it ended up in his jacket pocket? Maybe someone ought to ask Princess Nadine that question. He grabbed his denim jacket and put it on, then slipped the artifact back into the hidden, inside pocket, making sure it was secure.

"Thanks, Teddy," he said, picking the boy up and giving him a big kiss. "You're the hero tonight."

He got together the baby's things and he felt as though he were walking on air.

"Okay, Teddy," he muttered. "You're going to have to go back and stay with Caroline, because I'm going to get your mama back."

He knew he was supposed to wait for his brothers to go with him, but that was three hours away. He had to go now. Kayla was all alone and scared and he couldn't wait any longer.

Max had lived in Mercuria for almost a year and he knew all the little inlets along the coast and he could find them, even in the dark. He pulled his boat into a cove and tied it fast to a stand of pilings, then went ashore. It was a short walk to the castle. Mercuria was an old-fashioned country. The new, modern methods of security and border entry hadn't been introduced as yet. Very few people came to visit, because, after all, who cared about Mercuria? They had sat tight in their little isolated penin-sula for decades and most people didn't even know they existed.

Max knew certain passwords, certain door codes, and before long, he was in the central living area of the castle, smiling at his old friend Sven, doorkeeper to the royal family.

"Hey, Sven," he said.

"Max!" Sven, a big, burly Swede, stepped out to clap him on the back. "Hey, good to see you, old buddy. It's been a while. So you're back?"

"Ah…yes, I'm back."

"And you're going into the royal center?"

"If you're going to let me, yes, I am."

"You don't have a pass, I suppose."

"Do I ever?"

Sven laughed. "No, can't say that I've ever known you to arrive with the proper pass." He shook his head with pure affection. "Come on in. Shall I announce you to anyone?"

"No, thanks. I'm going to go in and see who's available. Hopefully, I'll find the king isn't busy and has time to talk to me."

"Oh, sure. I think someone said he's in the greenhouse right now."

"Okay. I'll just hang around until he gets back."

"Sure."

He'd given a lot of thought to where they might be holding Kayla. There was a guest room on the first floor, off the library. If they were being extra special nice, they might have put her there. He slipped around the kitchen where he overheard two kitchen maids gossiping, and headed straight for the library, then the guest room. Empty.

That left the women's jail on the second floor. He took the stairs, hoping he wouldn't pass anyone on the way, and came to the fortified area that had been built especially to hold female prisoners. He'd known a housemaid who'd been accused of stealing and had been kept there for weeks. He'd felt sorry for her, visited her often and finally won her release when the real culprit was identified. He knew the way in and the way out and he could pick the main lock at will. A few clicks and he was in.

Two cells faced each other, divided by a corridor between them. In one cell, just as he'd expected, there was Kayla, sitting on a bare cot and looking unhappy but otherwise unscathed. But what he hadn't expected was to find Princess Nadine sitting in the other cell, face muddy with the effects of a lot of heavy crying. She looked

up when Max entered, and her face bright-
ened considerably.

"Max," she said, jumping up and going
to the bars. "You came for me! Finally!"

But his attention was all on Kayla.

"Max!" She reached out her hand and he
took it in his, pulling as close to her as he
could.

"Are you all right?" Kayla asked anxiously. "How's your head?"

He'd forgotten all about his head wound.
He touched it gingerly. "It's okay. How
about you?" His gaze ran over every inch of
her, searching for any signs of wounds. She
looked a little mussed and had a bruise on
one cheek, which made him swear softly.
Her hair could use a combing. But she was
the most beautiful thing he'd ever seen.
"Did they hurt you?"

"No. Well, they did stick me with a tranquilizer dart."

He grinned at her. "Me, too."

She grinned back. "But other than that,
they've been okay."

"Max!" Princess Nadine called, sounding like the spoiled child she was. "Come see about me."

He looked over his shoulder. "Why is she in here?" he asked.

Kayla shook her head. "I'm not sure. I think her father put her in here as a sort of trap for you when you returned to get her."

"Get her?"

"They seem to think you two have a love affair going on."

"In her imagination, maybe."

"Or maybe her father is just mad at her."

"I'm not mad at all, young lady," said a deep, sonorous voice.

Max turned quickly. King Juomo was coming down the center aisle. Dressed in eighteenth-century royal garb of brocade and velvet, he looked splendid and ridiculous all at the same time.

"My daughter is incarcerated for a very specific purpose." He smiled and made a slight inclination of his head toward Max. "I'm glad you made it. We've been waiting for you. Now we can get on with things."

"Your Majesty, with all due respect, I

would like you to release Kayla right away. You have no right to hold her here. She has nothing to do with any of this."

He batted that pesky demand away. "I hear you're a prince now, my friend. What a lucky occurrence that is. Now my daughter will be doubly royal, won't she?" He put his head to one side, thinking hard. "Not to mention the unbreakable ties our two nations shall have with each other. Won't that be lovely?"

"Your Majesty," Max said bluntly, "I'm not going to marry your daughter."

"Oh, but I think you are. You see, I won't release your little friend here unless you do. It's quite simple, really." He smiled. "I've had the men in to fire up the old torture room in the dungeon. Quite a few nice old-fashioned machines in there. Can tear a body to ribbons, you know. I don't think your little friend will like it much. We will strive for historical accuracy, but still, her screams are going to be hard to take."

"Wait a minute." Max stared at the man as though he could hardly believe he was sane. "You're threatening to torture Kayla if I don't marry Princess Nadine? Are you crazy?"

"Not at all. I've been tested. I'm quite sane." He threw a dour look Kayla's way. "And not mad, either."

"I meant angry," she told him quickly. "Which is what I'm beginning to get. This is so absurd. I don't believe for a minute that you plan to torture me. You know very well international law forbids it."

He frowned. "Since when?"

"You don't keep up much with international affairs, do you? It's been that way for years. You can't get away with it. They'll string you up."

His laugh was jovial. "They'll have to catch me first."

"Really? And exactly where will you run to?"

He looked at Max. "I quite like your friend. She has a lot of spirit. Maybe I'll marry her myself." He giggled. "We'll have a double wedding."

"Daddy!" Nadine was sobbing.

"Hush, child. You wanted him and I told you I'd get him. Now he's here for you. Show a little gratitude."

"Tell you what," Max said sensibly, "I don't think anyone is marrying anyone at this point. But I do have a bargain for you. I might be able to produce your historical artifact."

"You'd certainly better produce the artifact. If you don't, you're all going to lose your heads."

"Oh, for heaven's sake," Kayla muttered just loud enough for Max to hear. "Now he thinks he's the Red Queen."

"If I can produce it," Max went on doggedly, "I'm sure you'll be gracious enough to let us both go free."

The king's eyes widened. "You and Nadine?"

"No. Me and Kayla."

He was frowning. "How does that help my little daughter? She loves you so."

"Daddy!" Nadine called.

"Hush. I'm negotiating here."

"But Daddy, I don't want him anymore. I hate him."

The king turned and glared at his daughter. "What?"

"I hate him. He didn't come back the way he was supposed to. I waited and waited."

"Well, he's back now. I went to a lot of trouble to get him for you."

"I know." She pouted. "I used to think he was really cute. But not anymore."

Max and Kayla exchanged significant glances.

"I don't understand," the plump man blustered. "I thought you couldn't live without him."

"Yeah, well…" She made a face. "He's not as cute as the new stable boy. Daddy? Please? I want the new stable boy."

Kayla grinned. By now she'd pretty much decided this whole thing was a thinly disguised farce. She couldn't believe anyone this silly could run a country.

"Maybe *I* ought to take a look at the new stable boy," she said brightly. "Who knows? Maybe I'll like him better, too."

Max turned to glare at her. He wasn't quite as ready as she was to assume this was an annoying but basically harmless situation. The king was off his rocker and pretty ridiculous, but that sort of person could go from farce to tragedy in a heartbeat.

But before he could say anything, there was a commotion in the hallway. There were shouts. A gun was fired, then another. And deadly silence.

They all stood very still, each holding his breath, listening for clues as to what this meant. Suddenly, the door to the cell room burst open and Monte appeared, with the guard Max knew as Sven in front of him with revolver pressed into his back.

"Your Majesty," Monte said to King Juomo, "so nice to meet you at last. We've come to take our people back, if you don't mind. The keys, please."

King Juomo seemed dumbfounded and very scared. Hands trembling, he produced the keys. David came in behind Monte and took the keys from him, opening the cell where Kayla had been sequestered and giving her a friendly smile.

"I always love it when they send in the cavalry," she noted approvingly.

"I don't know," Max said sardonically as

he looked around at his brothers, "I thought I was doing okay on my own."

"It never hurts to get backup," Joe told him. "And anyway, thanks for trying to cut us out of the action."

"How did you know?" he asked, quietly admitting to himself that he'd never been happier to see a gang like this show up on his side.

"Caroline called Kimmee. Kimmee called Pellea."

"And we figured the rest out on our own," Monte said.

Max shook his head and grinned at his brothers. Reaching into the pocket of his jacket, he grabbed the artifact and drew it out. "Here you go," he told King Juomo, handing it to him.

The king looked at his daughter. "So you were telling me the truth?" he cried.

She nodded sulkily. "I put it in his pocket for safekeeping. I wanted it to be with him always, wherever he went. I knew it would bring him back to me, one way or another." She sniffed. "And now I don't want him."

"You see what folly it was to do that?"

the king roared at her. "You see what trouble you caused?"

Her face crumpled but the princes were ready to leave her to her father's care and they began to head for the exit.

"It's been grand," Kayla said, saluting the king as she passed him. "Sort of like a visit to Freedonia without the Marx Brothers."

He looked rattled but it was evident he was starting to get color back in his face, and they hurried, not wanting to get bogged down in another discussion with him. Joe covered their departure, making sure the guards they'd disarmed on the way in weren't getting any ideas. And then they were on the boats and heading for home.

"There's something exhilarating about a good rescue operation," Monte said. "No casualties. Just some good clean fun."

"Fun." Max looked at Kayla, feeling drained.

She grinned at him. "All's well that ends well," she said.

Max groaned. "Another one of the quotes I'm supposed to learn, huh?"

She nodded and moved closer, putting

her head against his shoulder and enjoying the cool, clean spray from the ocean. She loved Max. And she was in love with him, too. It was a good day that taught you a life lesson that big. She meant to savor it.

In the morning, Max went to Kayla's to have breakfast with her and her baby. He sat eating a delicious breakfast pastry that Kayla had picked up at the bakery and drinking black coffee and listening to Kayla talk to Teddy and feeling as though he'd won the lottery. This was great. This made him a happy man.

Suddenly he realized something. It broke over him like a shooting star, spreading sparkling gobs of fire all around. Being a flyer was important, but not everything. Being a prince was going to be his life's work. But the one thing he really cared about above all others, the one thing he wanted to do with his life, was to protect Kayla, to protect her and cherish her and make her happy. And loving Teddy was a part of that.

He sat back and marveled at how simple it all was once he'd let himself break free of all the old hurts and fears. He'd spent much too much time tied up in knots of doubt. No more doubts. No more regrets. He loved Kayla. Therefore, he would live his life to honor her. And that was all there was.

Could he do that? Could he be a father? Why the hell not?

He looked across the table at the woman he loved. "Will you marry me, Kayla?"

She pursed her lips and pretended to be thinking it over. "I don't know. I'll have to think about it. There's a lot to consider." She searched his face and shook her head sadly. "If only you were as cute as the stable boy."

He groaned. "I'm going to trade you to King Juomo. You'll be happy there. He really knows how to treat a lady."

She grinned happily. "Okay, I'll marry you. Let's do it quick."

"Before we change our minds?"

"Never." She held her glass of orange juice up as a toast to him. "I'll love you forever, Max. Forever and everywhere and always."

"Me, too."

Teddy made a noise. It sounded very much like words.

Max frowned. "Did he just say, 'me, too'?"

Kayla nodded. "It sure sounded like it."

"You know what that means?"

"Tell me."

"We're a family now."

Rising from her chair, she went to slip onto his lap and put her arms around him.

"Sealed with a kiss."

* * * * *